The Dragons of Graham

by

Baird Nuckolls

Imagine Dragons!

Baird Nuckolls

The Wives of Bath Press

www.thewivesofbathpress.com

The Dragons of Graham © 2013 by Baird Nuckolls

This book is a work of fiction. Characters, names, places, events, and incidents either are the product of the author's imagination or are used for narrative effect, and may deviate from actual fact. Any resemblance to any actual persons, living or dead, events, or locations is entirely coincidental. If you find any real dragons at GMS, please let me know.

The Wives of Bath Press
223 Vincent Drive Mountain View, CA 94041
http:// www.thewivesofbath.com

Cover Art © 2013 by Jeff Monaghan
Edited by Heather Haven
Layout and book production by Baird Nuckolls and Heather Haven
Print ISBN 13: 978-0-9884086-1-6
eBook ISBN 13: 978-0-9884086-2-3

The Dragons of Graham

Dedication

To Caitlin and Grace, who inspire me to
look for dragons in unexpected places.

CHAPTER ONE
The Night Before

The summer zoomed by so fast Katie couldn't believe it was already over. Then today, time slammed on the brakes. It was only seven-thirty in the evening, it wasn't even dark yet, and tomorrow couldn't come soon enough. Katie bounced on the end of her bed.

"Sit still, Katie." Maia tugged the brush through Katie's shoulder-length brown hair.

"Ouch, that hurts."

"Well, if you'd sit still, it wouldn't hurt."

Katie was so excited, she couldn't stop bouncing. Tomorrow, she and Maia would be sixth graders. So tonight, Maia was braiding her hair.

"I don't see why you get to braid my hair, but I can't do yours."

"I'm braiding your hair so it will be all wavy tomorrow and it'll look cool. You know my hair never gets wavy." Maia flipped her long, dark hair over her shoulder. Her mother was Chinese, from Taiwan, and Maia had inherited her straight, black hair. It was thick and shiny, but it didn't get wavy. "I wish it would. I get so tired of it being straight. Maybe I should cut it off."

"What? No way. Your hair is too pretty." Katie was shocked. Maia had the most beautiful hair, like a black waterfall. She wouldn't care about braiding it, if her hair were like Maia's. "Besides, your mother would freak out."

"Probably." Maia finished the braid. "Hand me a hair tie," she asked, holding out a hand.

Katie fished around on the bed for the hair tie she'd been holding. "I wonder who we'll have for science? I've heard that Mrs. Mitchell is really strict."

"Yeah, they call her the Dragon Lady."

Both girls giggled just as the door opened. Katie's mom stuck her head into the room.

"Girls, it's almost time for Maia to go home. You have to get up early tomorrow, remember?" She frowned at the clothes lying on the floor. "What have you two been doing in here? It looks like a tornado went through."

"We were just picking out clothes for tomorrow, Mom."

"Well, make sure you put the rest away. You can only wear one thing at a time."

"All right, Mrs. Walker," Maia said, picking up a blue sweater from the end of the bed, "we'll put everything away." Maia had a way with moms. She never seemed to get into trouble.

"I'll call you when Maia's mother gets here." Katie's mom shut the door as the girls started putting the clothes back in Katie's closet.

"I can't wait to find out our schedules," Katie said. "I hope we have every single class together."

"It's gonna be great." Maia was as excited as she was. "Do you think we'll get into Spanish?"

Katie threw a pair of pink Converse into the back of the closet and closed the door. "You asked for it for your elective, too, didn't you?"

"Yup." Maia folded a pair of green pants and put them in a drawer. "I can't wait til tomorrow."

"Neither can I."

§

At seven-thirty the next morning, Katie walked down the sidewalk toward the Graham Sports Pavilion. She couldn't believe how many kids were milling around. Hundreds, maybe. How was she going to find Maia in this crowd?

"Hi, Katie." Josh Palmer, a boy she knew from Slater Elementary, came up beside her in the stream of students all headed in the same direction.

"Hi, Josh, have you seen Maia?"

"Not yet. Wow, can you believe this crowd? And it's just the pixies. The seventh and eight graders got their schedules last week."

"Pixies? What are pixies?" Katie was confused.

"That's what the older kids call the sixth graders.

They like to tease us for being short." Josh had an older sister in the eighth grade, so he would know.

The crowd squeezed through the gym doors. Inside, the high-ceilinged room was jammed with kids. The noise was amazing, like a riot at the zoo. Katie looked around for Maia's dark, shining head. There she was, on the bleachers. Katie said goodbye to Josh and headed in her direction.

The teachers were standing near the bleachers, herding the kids up into the seats. Katie worked her way up the steps to where Maia sat.

"I'm glad I found you. This place is crazy." Katie sat down next to Maia.

"I know; look at all these kids. I can't wait to meet some new people. I am so tired of having all my classes with the same thirty kids." She put her hand on Katie's arm. "Not you, of course, but some of those girls from Slater were driving me nuts."

A whistle blew and someone spoke into a microphone. It was the principal, Ms. Thompson. "Good morning, students. Welcome to the first day of school at Graham."

The kids cheered.

"We have a lot of things to do this morning, so we need your help. Over here," she pointed to the tables against the back wall, "are three stations. The first one is for gym uniforms, the second one is for library cards, and the last one is to get your schedule. Once you've gotten your things, please proceed to your homeroom class, which is also your first period class."

"This is so exciting." Katie started bouncing in her seat.

"Sit still. You're gonna make me nuts." Maia put a hand on Katie's arm.

"I'm already nuts."

"I know."

The girls watched the crowd, pointing out people they knew, as they waited to go down to the gym floor. Eventually, it was their turn to line up for uniforms.

"These things are awful." Maia held up the pair of red nylon shorts and grey t-shirt when she got them. "Why do we have to wear gym uniforms anyway?"

"I don't know. Maybe they like to make us feel stupid."

"Well, I know one thing. I'm not ever going to take a shower at school. It's bad enough we have to change in front of everyone. Did you see those locker rooms? No privacy at all."

"Yeah, I noticed that," Katie replied. "I just hope I don't forget my locker combination."

The line for library cards moved quickly. They signed a form, promising not to lose their cards, and then moved into the schedule line. Josh was in front of them.

"Hi Maia. I see Katie found you." His smile was wide. "How was your summer?"

"Good. How was yours?" Maia smiled back more shyly. Katie suddenly wondered if Maia liked him; she would have to ask her later.

"It was great. My family went white-water rafting through the Grand Canyon. You should have seen it. The rock walls went on forever and it felt like we'd gone back in time to the dinosaurs."

"That's silly," Katie blurted out. "There wouldn't be any dinosaurs in the Grand Canyon."

"Oh yeah?" Josh got angry. "Why not?"

Before Katie could answer, Maia stepped in, smoothing things over. "I think it's pretty cool that you got to raft through the Grand Canyon."

"Thanks." Josh beamed at her and turned around as the line moved forward. She turned to glare at Katie.

"What's with you? He was just being nice."

"He was just being dumb," Katie whispered back, rolling her eyes. "The Grand Canyon is a lot older than the dinosaurs."

"Maybe, but you don't have to be mean to him."

"What's the matter? Do you like him or something?"

"No, I don't like him or 'something.' I just don't think you should say stuff like that." Maia changed the subject. "I wonder if we'll get Mr. Mulkey for math? Stacey, you know, from soccer, lives down the street from him and says he's really cool."

Josh overheard and turned back. "Mr. Mulkey teaches seventh grade math. We'll either get Mr. McGee," he pointed to one of the male teachers who stood under the basketball nets, scowling, "or Ms. Bernaschina."

Katie was not looking forward to math; it was definitely her worst subject. She liked writing stories and even social studies was okay, but math. Yuck.

"I hope I don't get Mr. McGee. He doesn't look too friendly."

"Oh, don't let him fool you. My sister says he has the best sense of humor and he's always telling silly jokes in class," Josh said.

The line moved forward and each of them got their schedules. They walked over to the side of the gym to compare their lists.

"First period, Math." Maia read off her sheet.

"What? I have Science with Mr. Alberts. What about second period?" Katie said.

"Spanish, Mr. Gomez."

Katie groaned. She didn't have Spanish. Her second period class was Beginning Band, followed by Language Arts, Social Studies, Math and PE. "Here, let's compare."

They held their schedules up side by side. Josh was in Katie's Science and Language Arts classes. He was in Spanish and Social Studies with Maia, but Katie didn't have a single class with Maia, until PE. Katie's heart sank.

"How can we only have one class together?"

"At least we have one."

"But it's PE and it's last period."

"Yes, but I'd rather have PE with you, than without you." Maia shuddered. "The whole locker room thing gives me the creeps."

"And I didn't even get into Spanish." Katie whined. "Beginning band? Who's idea was that? I don't play anything and I can't even read music."

"Well, there are so many kids here, they have to put them somewhere." Josh was trying to be helpful, but it wasn't helping.

"But I thought Katie and I would be in all our classes together, so we could study together. It was going to be so much fun."

"We can still study together." Maia stuffed her gym uniform and her schedule in her backpack.

"I guess." Katie's feet felt made of lead as they headed out to their homerooms. They were grouped by last name and Huang was very far away from Palmer and Walker on the list.

"I'll see you at PE," Katie called to Maia as they split up.

"And break, and lunch. Won't be that long." Maia turned and went into Room 3.

It will be forever, thought Katie, as she and Josh headed to Room 23.

CHAPTER TWO
The Band Dragon

The sound coming out of the trumpet was like a dying cow. There were gasps and twitters around the room. Katie could hear Crystal and Sylvia behind her laughing and whispering. They were very amused by all of Katie's efforts, but she tried to ignore them. It was only the second week of school, but Katie was beginning to feel like she would never learn to play an instrument.

"Try it again, Katie," said Mr. Cassell. "This time, try to tighten up your diaphragm as you blow."

Katie pursed her lips and tried again. She wasn't entirely sure where her diaphragm was, but it didn't seem to matter. She couldn't make the trumpet sound right. The noise started with a whoosh and became a farting sound. The laughter behind her got louder.

"That's okay, Katie. Let me think about it for a bit. We'll find you the right instrument, don't worry. But for now, just sit here and listen to the lesson." Mr. Cassell was trying to be supportive, but Katie could see him wince every time she tried to play.

Beginning Band was not her idea. She didn't have a musical bone in her body. She and Maia had both wanted Spanish as their sixth grade elective, but only Maia got in. Katie got stuck in Band.

In fact, Maia had a great schedule, but the only class they shared was seventh period. They saw each other at break and lunch, but Katie wished they had more classes together. She and Maia had been friends since kindergarten; they played on the same soccer team and even went to the same orthodontist. At Slater Elementary, there was only one class for each grade and they knew everybody, but here at Graham Middle School, there were almost three hundred sixth-graders, "pixies" in school slang, and Katie felt lost in her classes. She didn't know hardly anyone.

Crystal and Sylvia had gone to Bubb and they were in a couple of Katie's classes, but they were already part of the popular crowd, so she didn't think they'd ever be friends. They just liked to gossip about everyone and everything. Katie was looking forward to seeing Maia at break and telling her about the latest musical catastrophe, but Mr. Cassell called her into his office just as the bell rang.

"Katie, I think you should try playing the flute. It looks

complicated, but it really isn't hard to make the notes. We can get you one from the band equipment closet and you can take it home and try it. Tomorrow's a block day, and you won't have band until Thursday, so you'll have some time to play with it. You can also bring it by at lunch tomorrow, if you're having any trouble, and I can help."

"Okay, Mr. Cassell. Do you mean we'll get it right now?"

"Sure. I just have to make a phone call first. I'll meet you there. It's the door on the left, across the courtyard."

They had fifteen minutes of break between second and third period every day. In elementary school, it was called recess, and everyone ran screaming to the playground, but here it was just enough time to get things from your locker, eat a snack, and visit with your friends. Katie was going to meet Maia half way between their third period rooms and catch up with their day, but she had to get the flute first. She looked for her as she walked across the courtyard, but didn't see her. Hopefully, this wouldn't take all of break.

After five minutes of waiting for Mr. Cassell, she started worrying. She wanted to see Maia and they only had a few more minutes before the bell rang. Maybe Mr. Cassell meant she should go in and find a flute herself. She tried the door. It was unlocked. The room was dark, so she flipped on the switch beside the door. Only one little bulb came on, near the front. There was no way to keep the door open, so when it swung closed behind her, it was pretty dark inside. Katie looked around. There were shelves in rows, with boxes of papers and black instrument cases on them. The ones closest to the door were big - probably trombones and French horns. She didn't see any little flute boxes.

She took two steps down the aisle and froze. There was a shushing sound coming from the back of the room. It made the hair on the back of her neck stand up. It didn't sound like the kind of noise that a machine made, more like something big sliding across the floor.

It was a bad idea to come in here alone. Katie turned and ran, slamming the door shut on her way out. By the time she reached the corner, looking for Maia, she felt silly. She probably just imagined the noise. There was nothing scary about the band equipment room. Before she found Maia, the bell rang. She dashed off to her next class, hoping not to get a late slip.

§

"Where were you? I waited the whole break." Maia said as Katie sat down at the lunch table.

"I had to get a new instrument from the band equipment room."

"What happened? I thought you were going to play the trumpet?"

"Yeah, I tried that, but I sounded like a dying cow. Crystal and Sylvia really had a laugh over it."

"Don't let them bother you, Katie. They don't really mean anything, I'm sure. So what are you going to try now?"

"Mr. Cassell wants me to try the flute."

"Oh, that should be cool. Did he give you one? Lemme see."

Maia looked at Katie's lunch box as if she was going to pull it out from underneath her sandwich.

"Um, well, I had to get it from the band equipment room, but Mr. Cassell never showed up." Katie paused, feeling a little embarrassed. "I finally went inside to look myself, but the room was really dark and there was a scary noise. So I didn't get it."

"What kind of noise?" Maia took a big bite of her apple.

"A shushing noise, like a snake moving, only much, much bigger."

"What do you think it was?"

"I don't know, but it seems kinda silly now. It was probably just my imagination. Will you come with me? We can go and get the flute together."

"Sure."

The girls finished lunch and headed to the band equipment room. The door was still unlocked and Katie had left the light on.

"Look at all these." Maia ran her hand over the row of black cases. "Does the school own all these instruments?"

"Yeah, they lend them to students to use. Do you see anything small enough to be a flute? I think it's about this big." Katie held her hands up about a foot apart.

"Not yet."

The girls walked further down the row between the shelves. The room was bigger than it looked from the doorway and it was very quiet. The dim light didn't carry all the way to the back.

"Maybe we should go and get a flashlight. It's dark in here." Maia walked around the last row of shelves and peered into the darkness. Suddenly, there was a flash of light and a sizzling sound. Maia screamed.

"What is it? Are you okay?" Katie came running and found Maia huddled against the wall.

"Look." Maia pointed into the corner. There, in the dim light, they could just make out a large shape. Something glittered nearby, on the floor. There was another hissing sound and another flash of light. In the glow, they could see the shape better. It was a dragon, sitting on a pile of band instruments. Both girls gasped.

He was dark purple and scaly, the size of an elephant. The glow was coming from his mouth. Not flames, exactly, but something that was bright when he opened his mouth to breathe. The hissing sound was definitely coming from him and there was a strange smell of burned rubber in the air.

Katie pulled Maia closer and whispered in her ear. "Does that look like what I think it is?"

"A dragon?"

"But...but dragons don't exist."

"I didn't think so either, but we're both seeing it, so it's not just your imagination." Maia took a deep breath. "What's it sitting on?"

"Band instruments, I think."

The glow from the dragon's mouth reflected off the shiny silver instruments on the floor. Trumpets and French horns, trombones and a few flutes. The dragon was sitting on a pile of them.

"Hey look, there's your flute." Maia pointed toward the dragon. "All you have to do is go get it."

Katie punched her. "I'm not going near that thing."

"Well, it's *your* flute. I'm not going to do it. Besides, it looks like maybe it's asleep." Maia pointed. The dragon's eyes did appear to be closed. Katie wondered if they glowed, too.

"Let's get out of here."

The two girls slipped down the aisle, holding their breath, and out the door. They grabbed their bags and ran for the blacktop.

They stopped, panting, behind the backstops.

Katie began giggling hysterically. She was afraid that if she stopped laughing, she'd start screaming. "I can't believe I was scared when I thought there was a little snake in there. OMG, did you see that thing? THAT'S something to be scared of."

"I know, huh!" Maia was laughing too. "That was unreal!"

"What do we do now?" Katie looked back in the direction of the band equipment room.

"Go tell Mr. Cassell?"

"What, that there's a dragon in the equipment room? I don't think he's going to believe that." Katie looked at her watch. "Oh no, the bell's about to ring. I'll talk to you about this in PE. We'd better go."

As Katie headed to her math class, she wondered what other surprises waited for her in middle school.

CHAPTER THREE
Ask an Expert

At the end of PE, Katie pulled Maia aside. "Will you come over this afternoon and help me figure out what to do?"

"About the thing in the band equipment room? No way. I'm not going back in there."

"Maia, I need your help." Katie lowered her voice. "I have to get that flute. Mr. Cassell told me to bring it in at lunchtime tomorrow."

"Why don't you just ask him to help you? He must know there's a dragon in there."

"I can't go up to Mr. Cassell and say, 'I'm afraid of the dragon in the equipment room, can you come with me?'"

"Why not?"

"I just can't." She was quiet for a minute. "We can figure something out. Come on."

The two girls walked to Katie's house. She only lived

half a mile from school. They said hello to Katie's mom, grabbed some cookies and went to Katie's room. Just as they were getting settled, the door burst open.

"Katie, Katie, look at this." It was Rosie, her little sister. Rosie was in second grade and she was a brat.

"Go away, Rosie." Katie turned her back, hoping that her sister would get the idea and leave.

"Look what I drew in school." She was holding out a piece of colored paper.

"What did you draw, Rosie?" Maia asked. She was always nicer to Rosie than Katie was. Katie just wanted Rosie to go away.

Rosie held out the drawing to Maia. It was a princess in a castle.

"Nice princess."

"Thanks, it's the princess Lisabeth. She's being held captive by a dragon who wants to eat her."

"Really? Where's the dragon?" Maia asked, winking at Katie, who turned to see at the mention of the dragon.

"Oh, he's in the dungeon, guarding his hoard."

"What's his hoard?" Katie asked.

"His hoard is a pile of gold. Dragons love gold."

"What about silver, do they hoard silver, too?"

"Yeah, sure. Gold, silver, jewels. All that stuff."

"What do you do if you want to take something the dragon is hoarding?" Maybe this would help with her problem.

Rosie thought about for a few minutes, her hand on her chin. Katie wished she would hurry up and answer; Rosie just liked to have them both paying attention to her. Katie was about to tell her to forget about it when Rosie finally answered.

"I think you could probably lure him away with something valuable, you know, but it would have to be something he wanted. Dragons are picky."

"What do you think would work?" Maia asked gently.

"Gold. They like that the best."

"Thanks, Rosie, for showing us your picture." Maia handed it back and looked at Katie.

"Yeah, thanks. Now scram." Katie pushed her out the door and pulled it closed. "Did you hear that? We need to figure out something that the band room dragon might want so we can lure him away from the instruments."

"Hmmmm." Maia looked around the room. "Maybe if we have something gold and shiny to use as bait." She saw a medal hanging from the bulletin board. Katie had gotten it when she won first place in a Soccer Kickoff. The medal wasn't real gold, but it was gold-colored and it was shiny.

"How about this?" She held it up for Katie to see. "We could show it to him, and then throw it across the room. While he went to get it, we could grab the flute."

"That's a good idea. Will you come with me in the morning?"

"I guess." Maia sounded reluctant. "I don't want to get too close to that thing, but I can't let you go by yourself. Okay, I'll come." She pulled up her backpack and took out her agenda. "Now, did you get as much math homework as I did? I gotta get started."

§

The girls agreed to meet at school a few minutes before the first bell. Katie brought the soccer medal and prayed that the band equipment room would be unlocked. She tested the door handle. It was open, but she waited for Maia. She didn't want to go in alone.

Maia came along a few minutes later. "Is it locked?"

"No, um...I..I was just waiting for you."

"Then let's go," Maia said.

"Um...wait." Katie was suddenly nervous. "What if the dragon's awake?"

"I guess we want it to be awake so we can lure it away from the pile. I brought a flashlight with me. Did you?"

"No, gosh, I forgot." Katie looked down at the medal in her hand, thinking maybe they should just forget the whole thing.

"That's okay," Maia said. "Mine should be enough. How about I go down the left side and shine the light on the medal? It should get the dragon's attention."

"Good idea." Katie handed the metal to Maia.

"Then, when he comes after it, I'll drop it and run. You go down the right side of the room and grab the flute. We both head for the door as quick as we can."

"You're not scared of him anymore?"

"Well, I thought about it a lot last night. I'm still scared, but I think if we move fast, we'll be okay. Besides, we're safer together."

"Then let's do this." Katie left her backpack outside the door. She didn't want anything slowing her down if she had a dragon after her. "Are you ready?"

"Yeah. I think so."

Katie pulled open the door and flipped on the light.

The room was as dim as it had been the day before. Maia put her finger to her lips and motioned for Katie to head to the right.

She went down the side of the room. Katie reached the last row of shelves and peeked around the corner. There was the dragon. He was even bigger than she remembered. His scales were the size of basketballs and looked like leather. His claws were wrinkled and black, like the feet of a parrot she'd seen once at the zoo, only much bigger.

He was sleeping with his mouth open. Katie could hear a soft roaring sound. He was almost snoring. The glow from his throat lit up the instruments under him. Katie wondered where the flutes were. She saw Maia peek around the left end of the shelves.

"Wait." Katie whispered. She didn't want to wake him up until she knew where the flutes where. "Shine your flashlight on the instruments so we can find the flutes."

Maia swept the beam across the floor. She was careful to keep it off the dragon.

"There, I see them." Katie pointed to the front of the pile. There were three flutes lying in a tangle with a trumpet. She would have to be quick. "Okay, go ahead. I'm ready."

Maia held up the medal with one hand and shone the

flashlight on it. It glittered in the dim light like real gold. She whistled loudly. "Hey, you. Dragon."

The dragon made a snuffling noise, but didn't move. They were going to have to try something more.

Maia looked around and then stepped closer to the shelves. They were made of metal. She banged her metal flashlight against them and the sound rang out in the small space. This time, the dragon lifted its head, looking around.

"Over here, Dragon." Maia shined the light on the medal again. "Come and get it." She swung the medal back and forth like she was trying to hypnotize him.

Katie watched the dragon closely. What if it didn't move? This was her only plan. What if it moved so fast that it grabbed the medal before she could get the flute? She hoped it wouldn't come after them.

The dragon stretched its scaly neck and yawned. Little tendrils of smoke and jets of flame came out of its mouth. It shook its head and turned toward Maia.

"Look here. I've got something for you." She dangled the medal in his direction. It swung slowly back and forth.

"Gold. Want some gold?"

The light from the flashlight reflected off the medal, bouncing gold spots around the room. The dragon reached out one long, thin arm, claws extended. But he couldn't reach the medal from where he was sitting. Maia took a step back.

"You can have it, but you have to come get it."

She held it higher and out to the side. The dragon stirred, stretching itself, taking its time. Katie's breath was caught in her throat. Why didn't it get up and get the medal? She bounced on her toes, ready to dash over and grab a flute.

The dragon stood up suddenly. It moved faster than Katie expected. Maia didn't do anything at first, when it got up, but then she tossed the medal into the corner and ran around the end of the shelves. This was Katie's chance. She dashed out of her hiding place and grabbed one of the flutes. It was caught between the valves of a trumpet, so she grabbed another one. She didn't have time to wrestle with it. This one slipped free, just as the dragon was picking up the gold medal. She spun around, careful not to trip over the instruments, and ran for the door. She didn't want to stay and see what he thought of his new prize.

As she got to the front door, it was just swinging closed behind Maia. She yanked it open again and rushed out, pushing it closed with her free hand as she went.

Maia was holding out her backpack; she grabbed it and ran. Maia followed. They stopped when they got around the corner. Maia was shaking, but Katie was excited. She started laughing.

"That was so awesome. Did you see that thing? He could have eaten you in one big bite."

"Don't remind me. Wow!" Maia took a deep breath, her hand over her heart.

Katie wondered if it was pounding as hard as hers was. "But it worked! I got my flute and now I can go to band class."

"Won't Mr. Cassell wonder why you don't have the case?"

"If he wants me to have the case, he can get it himself. I'm not going back in there."

The bell rang.

"Time for math. At least Mr. McGee isn't nearly as scary as that dragon. I'll see you at break." Maia shouldered her pack and left for class.

Katie walked to science class, holding her silver flute in her hand.

CHAPTER FOUR
The Shower Dragon

For the first two weeks of school, they didn't have to wear their gym uniforms, known as "dressing out" for PE. Today, they were starting soccer and Katie was afraid that Maia would be freaking out. She didn't like changing in front of anyone, even at Katie's house for sleep-overs.

When Katie got to the locker room, Maia wasn't there yet. The room was crowded with rows of dull red gym lockers and shelves just higher than her head. In between, were benches to sit on while you were putting on your shoes. The room smelled like old laundry and cleaning products. Katie put down her bag and started to change, when Crystal and Sylvie came in, talking loudly about something. They broke off their conversation when Maia came in right behind them, already in her uniform. Crystal looked at Maia and said in a very snarky voice,

"What did you do, wear your gym uniform under your clothes?"

"No, I changed in the girl's bathroom on the way over here."

Sylvie chimed in. "Mrs. Saunders said we have to change in the locker room. You're going to get in trouble, you know."

"Thanks for the lecture," Maia said, turning her back on them. She walked over to Katie. "Let's go." Katie finished tying her shoes and they ran outside. The field was bright green, surrounded by a springy red track. They stopped at the edge of the field to stretch.

"Are you okay?" Katie asked.

"I'm fine. Let's just play."

Katie loved to play soccer. She and Maia passed the ball easily between them, like they'd been doing for years. The sun was out and it felt good. The grass was green and smelled fresh. Katie wished for her cleats so that she could really run. By the end of class, they were sweating and laughing. But Maia's face fell as they walked back to the locker room.

"What about the shower room?" Katie pointed at the door behind them. "Nobody goes in there," she whispered.

"Nobody goes in there because it's gross. The paint is peeling and the floor is yucky. I don't want to change in there."

"I'll go in there with you, if you want. So you can have

some privacy."

"Okay, I guess so."

They gathered up their clothes and slipped into the room. The floor was dark gray, stained by something. At least there were little shelves in the shower stalls to put their clothes on. Maia stepped behind the curtain in the end stall. Katie went into one closer to the door.

As she was pulling on her socks, she heard a noise, like a bag of softball bats being dropped on the cement floor.

"Maia? Did you hear that?"

"No, I didn't hear anything."

"Um, let's get out of here. This place is creepy." Katie was beginning to think that coming in here was a bad idea.

"I'm almost dressed. Wait for me, will you?" Maia called, "I don't want to be here by myself."

"Yeah, I'll wait, but hurry." Katie listened for the strange sound. She pulled a water bottle out of her lunch bag and took a long drink. She was still hot from playing soccer.

She nearly dropped the bottle when Maia screamed. Katie rushed to the end stall and pulled back the curtain. Maia had backed into the corner of the shower stall. In front of her, hanging from the faucet head, was a long, blue-green scaly something, at least three feet long. It had four legs and tiny wings that fluttered madly as the thing reached out for Maia.

Its tongue flicked out of its mouth. Without thinking, Katie threw her water bottle at it.

The bottle hit it right behind the head. The thing dropped off the faucet and turned itself into a ball of scales. Maia jumped over it and ran for the door. Katie looked back and saw the thing, uncurled, sniffing out the water bottle and licking the puddle that had run out.

The girls dashed through the locker room and headed for the parking lot.

"What was that thing?" Maia screamed as they ran.

"I think it was another dragon, but I don't know what kind."

"Uuuggg." Maia shuddered as she slowed to a walk. "Thanks for saving me."

"My pleasure." Katie laughed. "No wonder no one goes in there. That was awful."

"Let's not ever go in there again."

"Okay. But I think we should go ask Rosie if she knows what kind of dragon that was. She seems to know a lot about dragons."

Katie linked arms with Maia and they turned down the street.

"And we seem to be finding them all over the place," Maia replied.

§

On the way home, Katie and Maia talked about their classes, but they didn't talk about PE or the dragons. It was really weird that they'd found two dragons, but now that they were away from school, Katie decided it was more exciting than frightening. Well, she was frightened of the one in the band equipment room, because it was so big. But the dragon in the locker room looked lonely. It might be more scared of them, than they were of it. Maybe Rosie would tell them more about it.

Rosie was in the bathroom when the girls got home. Katie knocked on the door. "Rosie, you in there?"

"Yeah, I'm busy."

Katie looked at Maia and rolled her eyes. "She goes in there and plays with her fairies and horses. I wish she'd just keep them in her room." She turned back to the door and knocked again.

"We need to talk to you, Rosie. Come on out."

"What about? I didn't touch your stuff."

"No, I didn't say you did." Katie sighed. Rosie was so annoying sometimes. You couldn't talk to her about anything important when you needed to.

"We have some questions about dragons." Maia called.

"Maia, is that you?" They could hear something rattle into a box and a drawer close. "I'll be right there."

Katie went into her room and dropped her backpack on the floor. Maia followed and sat on the bed. When Rosie arrived, she was carrying a large black and green book.

"What's that?" Maia asked her.

"*Dragons Through the Ages*. It has everything you need to know about dragons." Rosie showed them the cover, which had a drawing of a large jewel-colored dragon, wings extended, hovering in the air.

"Does it talk about any long, skinny dragons with blue skin?" Katie asked, reaching for the book.

Rosie pulled it back and went to sit on the bed beside Maia. "I'll look." She held the book in her lap so that Katie couldn't see.

Katie sighed. This was a mistake. They should just go to the library. Rosie was going to be difficult. Rosie continued turning the pages, looking for something.

"Hey, what's that?" Maia asked, pointing to a page.

"That's a Chinese dragon. They call it a Chinese Lung," Rosie tried to sound as official as she could. "They bring prosperity and luck."

"Looks just like the one we..." Maia started to say.

"...like the one we heard about," Katie interrupted. She didn't want Rosie to know that they'd seen one of these. Rosie was looking at the book and didn't seem to notice.

Maia looked down at the pictures and tried again. "What else does it say, Rosie?"

"It is a water dragon and it usually lives in a cave, but it can also hide in clouds."

"Yeah, or a shower stall," Katie muttered. "How big do they get?"

"Oh, the adults can be forty feet long."

Katie and Maia looked at each other. A forty-foot water dragon in the shower room was not something they wanted to see.

"Thanks, Rosie." Maia said. "See ya later."

After she'd left, Katie looked at Maia. "I was thinking it might have something to do with water, since it was in the shower. You didn't see, but it was really interested in my water bottle after I threw it at it."

"Maybe it was thirsty."

"Yeah, no one has used those showers in a long time. Maybe that's why it was in there. It needs water. What should we do about it?"

"Do about it? I don't know about you, but I'm never going into the shower room again."

Katie laughed, but she also thought maybe they should tell someone about the dragon in the shower. Maybe it needed help.

The next afternoon, she saw Mrs. Saunders outside the door to the girl's locker room.

"Mrs. Saunders, is there a reason we don't use the showers?"

"I think it's just a school policy, dear. We don't really have enough time for the students to take showers during class."

"So there isn't anything wrong with it?"

"With the showers, you mean? No, I don't think so. Now, hurry up and get changed. We have to get out to the field."

Mrs. Saunders walked away before Katie got the nerve to say anything more. Well, she'd just have to keep an eye out for the dragon herself.

CHAPTER FIVE
Manga Club

There were seven periods every day, along with break and lunch. They had just four minutes to change classes. There were so many kids at Graham, that the halls were very crowded, and it seemed like everyone was going in a different direction. Katie was late to class a couple of times; she felt like a salmon swimming upstream. One day, she discovered that if she walked right behind one of the taller eighth graders, she could follow in their wake and get to class faster.

One Tuesday, at the beginning of October, she was late getting to the spot near the library where she usually met Maia during break; no eight graders were conveniently going in the right direction. Maia was talking to a girl Katie hadn't met.

"This is Victoria. She's in a bunch of my classes."

Katie's stomach tightened. The girl was one of the group of 'populars' that hung out together during lunchtime. Crystal and Sylvia were part of that group, too.

"Hi, I'm Katie."

"Hi." Victoria glanced at Katie, then looked back at Maia. "So, are you interested?"

"She wants me to join the Manga club," Maia explained.

"What's that?"

"It's a group that meets during lunch on Thursdays, to talk about manga. You know, Japanese comics, anime." Maia sounded like she was already in the club.

"Yeah, we watch movies and draw our own manga cartoons. Sometimes we have competitions of our stuff." Victoria flipped her blond hair over her shoulder as she talked.

"Um, that sounds like fun." Katie wasn't sure what she should say. She looked forward to seeing Maia at lunch every day. If she was gone to some club, who would Katie eat with? Her smile disappeared.

"Oh, you should join, too." Maia grabbed her arm. "Let's go see where they meet."

The girls walked over to Room 27. Ms. Hess was an eighth grade Language Arts teacher who hosted the class. She waved at Victoria as they came in. "Hi, girls."

"Ms. Hess, this is my friend, Maia, and her friend, um, Karen. They want to join the Manga club."

Katie stared at Victoria. She was about to say something about her name, but Ms. Hess looked busy with the papers on her desk. She looked up at them for a second and asked, "Did you tell them our rules?"

"No, but I will." Victoria headed back outside. "See you Thursday."

Maia and Katie followed her. "What are the rules?" Maia asked.

"Oh, you just have to be on time, do your homework, and you can't be in the club if your grades go down. No big deal." Victoria linked arms with Maia and turned to go.

"See you later?" Maia called over her shoulder.

"Yeah, bye." Katie waved, as she watched them walk away. She hoped Victoria wouldn't be there at lunch. Things weren't going the way she expected this year. It wasn't just having so many different classes and teachers. She didn't really even mind all the homework, although it took way longer than she ever expected. It just seemed like Maia didn't have much time for her now. And there was Victoria, too. Katie just wanted to talk to Maia about all the dragons and what they should do about them, but she didn't want to include anybody new in that conversation. Maybe they would think she was crazy or something. She wasn't sure what she was going to do.

§

Maia wasn't waiting for her at their usual spot at lunchtime. Katie grabbed her lunchbox and walked over to the lunch quad. There was no sign of Maia or Victoria. She sat on the edge of a concrete planter to eat.

"Hi, can I sit here?"

Katie looked up to see Josh Palmer standing in front of her. He was holding his lunchbox in one hand and a carton of milk in the other. "Sure." She waved at the planter. "Plenty of room."

Josh was actually in more of her classes than Maia, but she hadn't really talked to him since the first day of school, when they got their schedules.

"So, what are you going to be for Halloween?" Josh asked.

Katie had a mouthful of turkey sandwich and took a minute to chew before she replied. "Oh, I don't think I'm going to do that this year. We're too old to trick-or-treat."

She and Maia had been vampires together last year, but she doubted that Maia would want to do anything this year. She hadn't said anything and they usually planned something by this time in October.

"Oh. Well, I'm going to be a Dalek." Josh put his carton of milk down on the ground and opened his lunchbox. He fished out a container and opened it. Inside were three rows of sushi rolls. Katie was surprised. He didn't seem the sushi type. After all, he was as plain old American as she was.

"What's a Dalek?"

"From Dr. Who, you know?" He ate the sushi rolls with a pair of wooden chopsticks.

"No, I don't know. That's a tv show, right?"

"Yeah, a science fiction show from the UK. The Doctor is a Time Lord and he travels around in a Tardis. That's a time machine that looks like a police box."

"A what?"

"Sort of like a telephone booth."

Josh was waving his chopsticks in the air as he described the Tardis. He seemed really into it.

"So what's a Dalek?"

"It's like a robot. They're a race of mutants from the planet Skaro and they want to exterminate anything and everything that's not a Dalek."

"That sounds....scary."

"Well, it'll make a neat costume. I've already made most of the parts."

"What does it look like?" Katie was having trouble imagining this mutant robot.

"Like a giant salt-shaker, actually."

That made Katie laugh. A giant salt-shaker didn't sound so scary after all. Just as Josh was going to continue explaining his Halloween costume, Katie saw Maia and Victoria walking down the far hallway. She jumped up and shoved her things back into her lunch bag.

"Sorry, Josh, I have to go...um...I have to talk to someone."

"Oh, bye." Josh called after her as she ran after the girls.

Katie caught up just as they were going into the classroom. "Maia, wait. Do you want to come have lunch with me?"

"Oh, hi Katie. Nah, I can't. I have to finish something for language arts. See ya later."

She pushed open the door and followed Victoria in, leaving Katie alone, again.

§

The Manga club met in Ms. Hess' room at lunchtime on Thursday. There were eighteen or twenty kids, mostly girls, already there when Maia and Katie came in. Maia waved at Victoria and hurried over to sit next to her. There were already two eighth-grade girls at the group of four desks. Maia sat next to Victoria, but there were no more seats, so Katie had to sit in the group behind them.

"Hi, everyone." Ms. Hess looked up from her desk. "We have some new girls today. Maia and Karen."

Katie raised her hand. "It's Katie, ma'am."

"Oh, I'm sorry. I thought Victoria told me your name was Karen." Ms. Hess looked from one girl to the other. Victoria just shrugged.

"She did, but it's really Katie." Katie felt awkward, but she felt she had to stand up for herself.

"Well, welcome, Katie." She turned toward the rest of the group. "Today, we're going to finish watching "The Cat Returns" and then afterwards, we'll talk about which movie to see next."

Most of the kids got out their lunches while Ms. Hess

turned on the movie. Katie had never seen it and she didn't have any idea what was going on. Maia and Victoria had their heads together, whispering, through most of the period. Katie couldn't hear what they were saying. She hoped Maia would tell her later. She sat and ate her lunch and tried to follow the movie.

The lunch period passed slowly. Katie felt really disconnected from the kids and the movie. She wasn't sure she wanted to be in the Manga club. She caught up with Maia on the way out.

"Wasn't that fun?" Maia said.

"It was okay, I guess."

"I'm so glad Victoria invited us. She said that the library has a big Manga collection. I want to go after school and check some out. Do you want to come?"

"Yeah...okay." Katie sighed. Manga didn't really interest her, but she didn't want to lose Maia, so she would go.

CHAPTER SIX

The Library Dragon

The library was around the corner from the office, on the way to the sports pavilion. It was sunny and bright and the books smelled so inviting. The librarians were really nice and always had suggestions of books they might want to read. It was open every day after school for thirty minutes and Katie liked to stop by sometimes. Her mom had said it was okay, as long as that she came right home after that. Mrs. Walker didn't want to worry.

Katie and Maia changed into their regular clothes after PE. Maia must have gotten more comfortable changing in the locker room with the other girls, because she changed without saying anything. Or maybe she'd decided that the water dragon was scarier than the rest of their class. Katie glanced at the door to the showers and wondered what had happened to the water dragon. Was it still in there, waiting for someone to turn the water on?

Maia saw her looking. "You're not thinking about going

in there, are you?"

"No, of course not." Katie shrugged. "I was just thinking about the 'you-know-what.' I wonder if it's okay?"

"As long as it doesn't come in here, I'm okay. I'm going to pretend it isn't hiding in there." Maia grabbed her backpack. "Let's go."

Katie picked up her pack and followed Maia out.

The fiction section was in the back of the library. The girls said hello to the librarian at the desk and made their way through the shelves to find the Manga.

"Victoria said the Manga is in the last row." Maia led the way.

Katie glanced at the books they passed, wishing she could stop and look at them. There were so many books here that she hadn't read yet. She couldn't wait to check some out.

Maia turned left at the last row. "You look down here and I'll look over there."

Katie stopped and pulled a book off the shelf. It was a Magic Treehouse chapter book. She remembered when she and Maia had been obsessed with them in the third grade. They read every one they could find.

The girls worked their way to the back corner of the library. They found the Manga books on the bottom two shelves. Katie reached down to take one, but the books were jammed so tightly together on the shelf that she couldn't get one out. She knelt down to get a better grip. With one hand bracing the row, she pulled hard on a single book to get it free.

"Ouch!" She rolled back, clutching her hand.

"What's the matter?" Maia bent down to see.

"Something...something bit me."

"Bit you? What are you talking about? Books don't bite."

Katie rubbed the back of her hand where there were two red marks. "No, but something did." She leaned forward to look at the shelf more closely. A set of black claws curled over the edge of the books. They were followed by a shimmering silver head. Katie sucked in her breath. "Um, hello?"

"What dooooo.... you want?" hissed a strange voice. It was like something out of an old movie. Maia scooted back against the opposite wall as the dragon slid out from between the shelves. It was much smaller than the shower dragon, with silver scales the size of quarters. It had a delicate face, with long eyelashes. Except for the fangs and claws, Katie didn't think it looked scary at all. She stepped in between Maia and the dragon.

"We want to read some Manga." Katie tried to sound confident.

"My booksssss," said the dragon.

"We just want to borrow them," Maia said from behind Katie. "We'll bring them back."

The dragon flowed across the floor and over one of Katie's tennis shoes. She tried not to flinch. Its breath was hot and smelled like something dead.

"I cannot borrow," the dragon said, "so youuuuuu cannot borrowwwww." His voice was sad.

"What do you mean?" Katie asked.

"No carrrrrrd."

"You need a library card?" Maia sounded surprised.

"Yesssssss."

Katie had an idea. "If we get you a library card, will you let us borrow the Manga books?"

"Possssssssiblyyy." The dragon was swishing his tail like an angry cat.

"Okay, we'll just go do that." Maia stood up, grabbing Katie by the arm, and pulled her away. She headed for the library door and kept going.

"That was too creepy for words. I've had enough with these dragons." Maia was moving so fast that Katie had to run to keep up. "I'm going to talk to Ms. Hess about this."

"Wait, Maia." Katie grabbed her arm and pulled her to a stop. "Don't."

"Don't what?" Maia was still very agitated.

"Don't tell Ms. Hess...about the dragon."

"Why not? That thing is dangerous. If you don't want me to tell Ms. Hess, then I'm going to talk to the librarian about it."

"Um, I don't think he was going to hurt us," Katie said. "I just think he's sad."

"Why, because he doesn't have a library card? Who cares? Besides, how the heck are we going to get a library card?" Maia finally sounded less mad. "We can't just walk up to the desk and say, 'Hi, we need a library card for a dragon in the Manga section.'"

"I know that. But we can try and make him something. Maybe he'd accept something that looked like a library card. We tricked that dragon in the band equipment room with my soccer medal, remember?"

"And what are you going to put on the card? Library Dragon? You don't even know if that thing one has a name."

"Maybe it's listed in that book Rosie has. Come home with me and we'll see if we can find out." Katie didn't want to ask her sister to help, but maybe they could just look at the book and not tell her why they needed it. "I need your help,

Maia. Please?"

Maia softened; she didn't seem too mad anymore.

"Okay. But then I have to get some homework done."

CHAPTER SEVEN
Library Card

"Do you see that dragon book?" Katie whispered to Maia as they looked into Rosie's room.

"No. Wasn't it dark blue?"

"I thought it was green." Katie walked in and lifted up a scarf that was draped over a chair. It was one of hers that Rosie had borrowed without asking. She stuffed it into her pocket.

"Why are we whispering? She isn't here." Maia bent over the bookcase at the end of the bed.

"Yes, I am."

Both girls jumped. Rosie was standing in the doorway, her hands on her hips. "Looking for something?"

"Yeah, we were looking for that dragon book." Katie felt a little guilty about being there uninvited, but Rosie *had* taken her scarf.

"Why?" Rosie's eyes narrowed.

"I just wanted to look at it." Katie looked around, hoping to see the book so that she could grab it and go.

"Well, if you'll tell me what you want to know, I can help you find it." Rosie walked over to her bed and sat down. She reached under her pillows and pulled out the dragon book.

Katie sighed. "We need to know the name of another dragon."

"Really?" Rosie's eyes grew wide. "What kind?"

"We don't know," Maia said.

"What does it look like?"

"It's silver and it has black claws." Katie rubbed her hand. "And sharp teeth."

"Is it shaped more like a snake or more like a big dog with wings?"

"A snake. What difference does it make?" Katie was getting annoyed.

"It just does. How many toes?"

"Toes? Gosh, Rosie, I have no idea. The darn thing bit me when I tried to take one of its books. I wasn't standing there counting its toes."

"Bit you? You mean, you've seen this dragon?" Rosie

jumped up and tried to look at Katie's hand, but she shook her off. Rosie turned toward Maia, instead. "See, if it had five toes, it was a Chinese dragon, four toes means Korean, and three toes means it's Japanese."

"If I had to guess, I'd say three." Maia smiled at Katie over Rosie's head. She was always good at settling down their arguments.

"That would make it a Japanese dragon." Rosie said.

"Okay, okay, so it was a Japanese dragon." Katie was still annoyed with her sister. "What can you tell us about it? Can you tell us its name?"

"Let me see." Rosie started to flip through her dragon book, stopping at one page and then another to read what was written there. Katie turned and paced across the rug.

"First, I can tell you that Japanese dragons are very wise, but they are also pretty cranky. You have to be very respectful of them, tell them how much you appreciate them. Otherwise, bad things might happen."

"What kind of bad things?" Maia asked.

"It says here 'natural disasters'."

"We don't want any of those. Do you know any names?"

"One of them was Ryujin. He was the king of the sea. He lived in a court of sea turtles and jellyfish."

"I didn't see any turtles and the library isn't under water. What else?" Katie tried to move the conversation along.

"There's Yofuni Nushi. He liked to eat human flesh and once a year he demands a maiden sacrifice."

"Oh, I hope he's not that one." Maia laughed.

"I know that Kinryu was a golden dragon, but you said this one is silver, right?"

"Right." Maia and Katie answered at the same time.

Rosie looked through the book for a long time, flipping pages back and forth. Katie tried to look over her shoulder, but Rosie just closed the book. Katie sighed. She really just wanted to figure it out, but making Rosie mad was going to make it take longer.

"I'll be right back. Do you want a snack, Maia?"

"Sure, whatever."

"Me, too," called Rosie as Katie walked down the hall.

"Yeah, okay." Katie came back a few minutes later with toasted English muffins covered in Nutella, her and Maia's favorite snack.

"I don't like Nutella," Rosie said, when Katie handed her one.

"Too bad, more for me." Katie took it back and took a big bite and Rosie stuck out her tongue at her. "Did you find anything?" Katie mumbled, her mouth full of Nutella.

"Well, there's one called 'O Goncho' that's white and signifies famine."

"That doesn't sound right." Katie swallowed her bite and continued. "We have to find the right name. I have a feeling he won't let us near the books, otherwise."

"You might call him 'Fuku Riyu' which is the Japanese dragon of good luck. He might like that." Rosie suggested.

"Will you write that down?" Katie asked, between licks of her chocolate-covered fingers.

"Sure." Rosie glared at Katie, but took a pencil and made some notes on a slip of paper. She gave it to Maia, who stuck it in her pocket.

"Thanks, Rosie. See ya later."

§

Friday morning, Katie met Maia outside the library before the first bell. "I have the names," Maia said, holding the slip of paper from Rosie.

"And I brought my camera." Katie had a little camera that made instant miniature pictures, the size of postage stamps.

They thought they'd get the dragon's picture, find out its name and then make a library card. It seemed like a good plan, but they only had about ten minutes before the first bell.

Katie got the camera out of her backpack as they walked back to the Manga section. Maia bent down and looked at the shelf where the dragon had been the day before.

"I don't see it."

"What should we do now?"

"Try whistling," Maia suggested.

"What good will that do?" Katie didn't think it would come, like a dog.

"I don't know. But it might work. Try it."

"Okay." Katie only knew the song from the Andy Griffith show that she watched with her parents on TV. She tried whistling it softly, but nothing happened. "Why don't you try something?"

"Like what?"

"You could be the one to try and pick out a book." Katie rubbed her hand where the dragon had nipped her yesterday.

Maia looked at her sideways, but she cautiously pulled on one of the Manga books. Just as the book started to slip out of the tightly packed shelf, the dragon appeared, flowing over the top of the books and down onto the floor at their feet.

"Yooooouuuu agaaaaaiiiinnnn."

"Yes, sir, Mr. Dragon." Maia had backed away and was standing behind Katie. "We just had a few questions."

"Yeeeesssss?"

"We have to know what name to put on the library card," Katie said. "Is your name...uh...uh" She looked at Maia and whispered "What did Rosie say?" Maia took out the piece of paper and handed it to her. "Um....is your name O Goncho?"

The dragon began to hiss and thrash its tail. "Noooooo."

Katie fumbled with the piece of paper. Rosie had circled this one. "Is it 'Yofuno Nushi'?

The dragon roared at this name and Katie froze. She looked toward the front desk. She didn't want the librarian to come and investigate all the noise.

"Do I loooooook like I want to eeeeeat you?" The dragon asked.

"No, no, I'm sorry, I know that's not right. You are a very wise and respected dragon. You wouldn't eat anyone."

The dragon looked slightly less angry. Katie looked at the paper. "Maia, what does this one say?"

Maia bent over the paper. She whispered the words in Katie's ear.

"Oh right, Fuku Riu." Katie looked at the dragon. "Is your name Fuku Riu? Your scales are so beautiful, you must be the Dragon of Good Luck."

The dragon stopped whipping its tail against the shelves. Katie swore that it might even be smiling. She must have said the right thing.

"Yeeesssss."

"Can I take your picture, Mr. Riu?"

Katie pulled the camera out as the dragon lifted its head. She snapped the picture, hoping that it would come out clearly the first time. The camera whined and the slip of a picture slid out. She peeled back the front of the paper to see the image develop. Silver scales and fearsome white teeth. Close enough.

"Thank you, sir. We'll be back with your library card as soon as we can." Katie put the picture in her jacket pocket and the girls walked away as fast as they could. Katie's heart was pounding.

They had planned to make a photocopy of a library card for the dragon's card, but one of the librarians was using the machine. They stood off to the side, waiting, until the first bell rang.

"We better get to class," Maia said, shouldering her backpack.

"Will you meet me back here at lunch to finish this?"

"I told V I'd meet her for lunch today. Can't you do this

on your own?"

"Please, Maia. It'll only take a few minutes. Then we can go and find Victoria together."

"Okay. I'll see you then."

§

At lunchtime, Katie walked toward the library to meet Maia. As she headed down the hallway, Josh came around the corner and fell into step beside her.

"Where are you going in such a hurry?"

Katie was a little surprised. They hadn't talked since Tuesday, when he ate lunch with her. She wanted to talk to him, but she didn't have time. She wasn't ready to explain about the dragons, and it would be really awkward if he followed her into the library.

"To the library, to meet Maia."

"Something more important than a well-balanced lunch?" he asked, laughing weakly at the joke.

"Um, no. Just something we have to do." Katie hoped he would take the hint and leave. Josh continued to follow her right up to the library door. She stepped through quickly and turned to him.

"Well, see you later." She waved and then shut the door. Maia was waiting at the copier.

"Who was that?" she asked.

"Oh, just Josh Palmer." Katie didn't want to talk about him to Maia. She might jump to conclusions. "He was just saying hi. He's in a couple of my classes."

"Is he following you around? Maybe he likes you?" Maia grinned.

"No, nothing like that. Come on, let's get this done." Katie put her library card down on the copy machine and covered it up with a math worksheet, in case any of the librarians were watching.

They took the copy out to the lunch tables and cut out the parts of the card with the library name and number on it. Maia wrote the dragon's name on a tiny slip of paper and they glued it over Katie's name on the copy. Then they attached the tiny picture they'd taken. The last thing to do was to cover the whole thing in clear tape, so that it looked like an official card.

"That looks pretty good," Maia said, turning the card over and checking the edges. "Let's see what the dragon thinks."

They went back to the library and headed to the Manga section. "Hello, Mr. Riu," Katie called. The silver dragon came slithering out of the books this time without further prompting.

"Yesssss?" the dragon looked at them with bright eyes. "Do you havvvvvvve something for meeeeee?"

"Yes, Sir. Here is your library card." Katie handed him the card proudly. He took it with one black-clawed hand.

"Ahhhhhhhhhh, goooooooodd." He held it close to his face and it looked like he was smiling again.

"Can we borrow some Manga now?" Maia asked.

"Yesssss." He slipped back behind the row of books as the girls picked out a few. "Help yourselffffff."

They checked the books out and walked toward the blacktop.

"Okay, I'm done with dragons, Katie," Maia said. "I don't want to discover any more of them."

"Oh." Katie was confused. She didn't want to make Maia mad, but she really thought the dragons were cool. "Are you scared of them? Because I don't think you need to be."

"No, I'm just tired of jumping out of my skin whenever I least expect to see one of those things. So, if you find any more, don't tell me about it."

They had always shared everything before, but since the beginning of school, Maia seemed to be moving away from her. She was doing more stuff with Victoria, like this

Manga Club, things that Katie wasn't that interested in. She agreed not to mention the dragons anymore; she didn't know what else to do.

CHAPTER EIGHT
The Egg

By the end of October, it was getting colder in the mornings, but it was still hot in the afternoon. Katie needed a jacket on the way to school, and she was glad that her mom had gotten her a Graham sweatshirt. By break, though, it was too warm to wear. She had to carry it around the rest of the day, which was a pain. She wished she had a locker to leave it in. Lockers were hard to get at Graham. There weren't enough to go around, so there was a lottery every year at the beginning of school. Both Katie and Maia had put in a request for one, but only Maia won one. That seemed to be how the year was going; Maia got everything she wanted and Katie didn't. But Maia gave her the locker combination and told Katie that she could use it, too.

One day at lunch, Katie met Maia at her locker when she went to get her lunchbox.

"Hey, Katie. Can you take some of this stuff home? I told Victoria that she could use the locker, too, and we need to make more room."

"What stuff?" Katie was instantly worried. There was barely enough room for her books and lunch, along with Maia's stuff. There really wasn't room for Victoria to share unless they took almost everything out.

"Oh, can't you keep some of these books in your backpack? Or your lunchbox?"

Katie looked at the locker. "I guess I could." She didn't really want to take any of it out. She needed the books for class and besides, she was Maia's best friend. She should have first shot at the space in the locker. "I'll take some stuff out this afternoon."

"That's great. I'm walking home with Victoria today, so I'll tell her she can start leaving her things there in the morning." Maia walked off toward the cafeteria. Katie shifted a few books around and stared glumly at the rest. Maia seemed to be spending more and more time with Victoria and Katie felt like she didn't know her anymore. Or understand her. It hurt. They had been such good friends and now she seemed to care more about Victoria and what the populars thought of her, than she did about Katie.

After school, she stopped at the locker again. It was a warm, sunny afternoon, and the trees between the classrooms were losing their leaves. Katie liked to kick around the large, dry sycamore leaves; they rustled and gave off a musty fall smell. The hallways were empty this afternoon. She could hear some kids running around on the blacktop, but everyone seemed to have cleared out of school pretty quickly today. She stopped in front of the locker and undid the lock. The locker was really full of stuff.

Maia's lunchbox was gone, so she must have already left with Victoria. Katie pulled her own lunchbox out of the locker and then sat down in front of the open door. She lifted out a few of Maia's notebooks, which were shoved into the space haphazardly. There was no order to it. If they kept things neater, there might be room for all three girls to use the locker.

Maia's books were mixed in with Katie's. She pulled two out and saw that the others weren't lying flat. Lifting up one more, Katie saw something round in the bottom of the locker. Was Maia keeping a basketball in there? No wonder there wasn't any room. Katie took all the books off the ball. But then she realized that it wasn't a ball.

It was flat on one side and it was a curious color, mostly black with swirls of dark red. What the heck? She reached for it and then jumped back. It was *warm*. A shiver ran up her spine. Something was very wrong with this thing in Maia's locker. She shoved the books back in and shut the door.

On the way home, she kept thinking about the ball in Maia's locker. Except it wasn't a ball. Maybe it was an egg? At home, she went into Rosie's room and picked up the *Dragons Through the Ages* book. Dragon eggs were oval and hard. According to the book, they needed to be kept warm, and when the dragon hatched, it would imprint on the first dragon it saw. From the pictures, Katie guessed that this was the egg of a Red Dragon, They were enormous things from Wales, called 'Y Ddraig Goch.' She had no idea how it ended up in Maia's locker. She wanted to call Maia and ask if she knew about it, but she was probably at Victoria's house and Katie didn't have her number. She would just have to ask her about it in the morning.

§

Katie found Maia outside her homeroom class the next day. She and Victoria were deep in conversation.

"Maia, hi. I need to talk to you."

"What is it, Katie? I have to get to class and Victoria needs the notes from Spanish."

"Well, it's about the locker."

"Yeah, did you take some stuff home?"

Katie looked over at Victoria, who was standing behind Maia, listening.

"I did, but I found something that might be yours. I didn't know."

"What was it?" Maia didn't sound very interested. She sounded distracted.

"Um...." Katie didn't really want to talk about the dragon egg in front of Victoria. "Can we talk alone?" She nodded toward Victoria, hoping that Maia would get the message.

Maia sighed and looked at Katie with raised eyebrows. "Yeah, okay." She followed Katie across the sidewalk.

"I found an egg," Katie said, keeping her voice low.

"Eew. Did you throw it out?"

"No, not that kind of egg. A dragon egg." Katie leaned closer to Maia's ear so that no one else could hear. "I looked in

Rosie's book and I think it's a Red Dragon egg. I don't know when it's going to hatch."

"Hey, let's show it to Victoria before you get rid of it."

"No."

"What?"

"No, I don't want to show it to Victoria, and I don't want to get rid of it yet."

"Katie, we have to get rid of it. I can't keep that thing in my locker."

"Just a couple days, Maia. I think it's about ready to hatch. And I have an idea."

"Then why can't we show it to Victoria? Does it look cool? Or is it all slimy and gross?"

"No, it not slimy, it's warm and dark and shiny. I just want to keep this whole dragon thing between us. Our secret."

"I don't like keeping secrets from Victoria."

Katie didn't know what to say. She felt that if Victoria knew about the egg or the dragons, then the story would become gossip all over the school. Or worse, kids would make fun of her and tease her for seeing things that didn't exist. She didn't trust Victoria or the populars at all.

"Okay, I'll get rid of the egg; just don't say anything to Victoria."

"What is the problem with you and V? I keep trying to include you in everything, which isn't all that easy, if you want to know. The rest of V's friends think you're kinda creepy; I keep telling them you're okay, and then you go and act all weird and secretive again."

"Why do you hang out with them, anyway? All they do is gossip and say mean things about people behind their backs."

"No, they don't. You don't understand. Besides, they're my friends."

"I thought I was your friend," Katie said, softly.

"Yeah, well, I'm not so sure any more." Maia turned away and went back to Victoria. Victoria said something to Maia that made her laugh and they giggled as they walked off together. Katie watched Victoria look back over her shoulder and smile at her. It was a mean smile.

Katie ran to class before anyone could see the tears in her eyes.

§

At break, she went to the office and found a large plastic bag. She got the egg out of Maia's locker. It was a lot heavier than she expected and it was hard to carry. She rolled it into the bag and managed to get it up and into her arms. She felt like everyone was watching her balance the egg and her backpack, as she walked toward the gym.

Just as she got to the edge of the field, the egg started to rock and shake. It was moving so hard, she couldn't hold on to it; the egg fell to the ground and rolled under a bush. It was hatching! Katie pushed the egg behind the bush so that no one could see it, and crouched beside it to watch.

First, a crack formed in one little spot, and then it started to crack around the egg in a circle. Katie saw a little claw come out of the hole. Suddenly, she remembered the warning in the book. The baby dragon would imprint on the first person it saw. That was the last thing Katie needed: a baby dragon who thought she was its mother.

She snatched the bag out from under the egg and pulled it over her head. Maybe that would be enough to confuse it. The egg kept rocking and the crack got bigger and bigger until finally, a big piece of the shell fell away.

The first thing Katie saw from under the bag was a scaly, red nose. It sniffed the air and turned its head toward Katie. Uh oh, she didn't want it to get any ideas. Katie moved around behind the next bush, so she wasn't as close. Maybe it couldn't smell her from there. The dragon went back to chipping away at the really hard shell.

As each little piece came off, more of the baby dragon emerged. It was a dark red color, with a long nose and funny feathery bits on the back of its neck. The tip of its tail had the same feather bits on it. She had no idea dragons would have feathers. Maybe it was just a baby dragon thing.

When it was finally done cracking open the egg, the dragon stopped and stretched up. Its neck was really long and its head stuck up over the top of the bush, even though it had tiny, little legs. She had to think of something quickly or the dragon was going to head out onto the field, and then everyone would see it.

Katie remembered that she had her lunchbox in her backpack. Maybe the dragon was hungry? She took out the tuna-fish sandwich her mother made her for lunch and tore off a small piece. She tossed it toward the baby dragon. The dragon's head swung around, and it sniffed the ground, until it found the piece of sandwich. It nosed it, but didn't eat it. Maybe it didn't like tuna fish?

She had some grapes in her lunch, too. She pulled one off and tossed it next to the piece of sandwich. The baby dragon's tongue flicked out of its mouth and surrounded the grape.

The next thing she knew, the tongue was gone and so was the grape. So that worked. Now she had to figure out what to do with the dragon. Just then, the bell rang; she had to be in class in four minutes. She had to hurry.

Most of the kids were headed toward their classrooms and Katie hoped that no one would notice her back here, leading a baby dragon toward the gym with a trail of grapes. It followed behind slowly, its tiny claws clicking on the pavement, slurping up each grape as it came across it. Katie didn't dare take the bag off her head. She had no idea how long the bonding thing went on. She just hoped that she'd get to the locker room before she ran out of grapes.

In fact, she only had one left when she led the baby dragon into the shower stall. Her plan was to introduce the baby dragon to the water dragon. She got out her water bottle and poured some on the ground. The baby slurped up some of the water and then Katie heard the same "bag of bats dragging" sound that she'd heard the first time they saw the water dragon. She didn't have much time.

The late bell was about to ring. Katie threw down the water bottle, and the rest of her tuna sandwich, and hoped for the best. She heard a small cry and an answering rumble as she ran out of the locker room. They would be all right.

CHAPTER NINE
Missing Maia

The next morning, Katie found Maia and Victoria at Maia's locker. Katie hoped that Maia wasn't still mad at her; she wanted to tell her about the baby dragon.

"Did you clean it out?" Maia demanded.

"Yes, I did."

"Good, because Victoria wants to put her stuff here." Maia turned away and started helping Victoria unload a bunch of books from her backpack.

"Um....Maia. Can we talk?" Ever since the egg hatched, Katie had been worrying about the baby dragon. She couldn't wait until PE to check and see if it was still there in the shower room.

"Not right now," Maia said, "We have to meet with Ms. Standley about our project."

Victoria didn't even look at Katie, as if she were invisible.

"Come on, V."

The girls walked away, arms around each other, leaving Katie standing at the locker. Katie stared after them. Did this mean that Maia wasn't her friend anymore. Her chest hurt just thinking about it. She got her books out of the locker and went to class.

§

The rest of the day was difficult. Katie had a hard time concentrating. In Science class, she couldn't remember the layers of the earth's crust that came up on the pop quiz. Mr. Alberts asked her a question when she wasn't paying attention and she completely flubbed the answer. She had been too busy wondering if Maia would be around during the break or if she and "V" were avoiding her. And what about the baby dragon? Maybe she should take some food over there. She didn't even know what baby dragons ate. When the bell rang at the end of Band, she went looking for Maia, but she wasn't in any of their usual places. Neither was Victoria. Katie ran into Josh as she was wandering around.

"Hi," he said, falling into step beside her. "Looking for Maia again?"

Katie stopped and turned to look at him. "What do you mean, again?"

"Oh, you're always with Maia or you're looking for her."

"We're best friends. Is that a problem?"

"No, I was just asking."

Katie slumped down on the closest planter box. "I seem to spend more time looking than anything. She's always off somewhere with V."

"Who?"

"Victoria."

"Oh. Are you friends with Victoria, too?"

"No." Katie stared at the ground.

Josh changed the subject. "So, what was up in science? You seemed upset. You still seem upset."

"I'm just worried about a bunch of things."

"Like what?"

Katie wondered if she could tell Josh about the dragons. After all, Maia didn't care anymore and it would be nice to have someone to talk to about them.

"What do you know about dragons?"

"You mean, like Dungeons and Dragons? Or like the ones in the Hobbit that breathe fire?"

"More like the fire-breathing kind."

"Not much, why?"

"What would you say if I told you I'd seen one? Or more than one?"

"You're kidding, right?"

"Nope."

Josh just shook his head and looked at her like she was strange. How could she prove it to him?

"Meet me at lunchtime and I'll show you something."

"OK. I have PE before lunch."

"Great, I'll meet you in front of the sports pavilion."

The bell rang to signal the end of break.

"Let's go," Josh said, standing up. "We're going to be late for Language Arts. You know how much Ms. Morrison hates it when we're late."

Katie laughed. "Yes, I do." She pulled the strap of her backpack over her shoulder and took off running, right behind Josh.

§

The next hour and a half passed too slowly, like waiting at the dentist's office. Katie had a knot in her stomach. Suddenly, she wasn't so sure it was a good idea to tell Josh about the dragons. Maybe he would stop talking to her, like

Maia had.

As soon as the bell rang, she ran to the gym. She wanted to check and see if the baby dragon was still there, first. She was so worried about it. Josh couldn't go into the girls' locker room, but she could take him to the library and see if the Japanese dragon was around. If not, there was always the band equipment room, but it might be locked. There had to be some way to prove that there were dragons at Graham. She realized she didn't want Josh thinking she was making it up.

She slipped into the girls' locker room through the side door. The water bottle she'd put in the last stall of the showers had been shredded into little bits. She checked each of the stalls and looked around the main locker room, too, but there was no sign of either dragon. Katie took out her sandwich and another water bottle and left them both in the corner of the shower. It was the best she could do. She left through the lobby and found Josh waiting out front.

"Come on, I have something to show you."

Josh just smiled and followed her to the library. The tables were full of kids reading during lunchtime. They walked quietly to the back corner. Katie reached down to pull out a few Manga books, a little afraid she might get scratched by the Japanese dragon again, but there was no sign of him.

She even crouched down to look behind the books, but she didn't see anything.

"What am I supposed to look at?" Josh was standing above her, looking down. He looked really tall from this angle.

"Um, there's a dragon who lives here and guards the Manga section, but he's not here right now. In fact, I haven't seen him since we made him a library card."

"A library card?" Josh looked confused.

"Never mind. Come on, I know another place to look."

Josh followed her to the MUR courtyard.

"There's another dragon living in the band equipment closet. He sleeps on a pile of silver band instruments." Katie pulled on the door handle, but it didn't budge. The door was locked.

"O...K..." Josh was smiling at her, but it was a 'you're being weird' smile, not a 'this is cool' smile.

"Look, I'm not making this up. I really have seen several dragons here at Graham."

"Katie, I want to believe you, but I don't know." Josh was backing away now, like she was crazy and it was contagious. Just then, the warning bell rang. "Gotta go."

Josh turned and took off for his class.

Katie was speechless. Now she'd done it. He would probably tell everyone that she was nuts and seeing things.

That's the last thing she needed. Her eyes pricked with tears. She suddenly wanted to run out of school and go home. But that would probably just get her into more trouble. She heard the late bell ring. Now she was going to have to sneak back into class.

The walkways between the buildings were deserted. Katie walked quickly, without running, toward her math class. Just as she was about to turn the last corner, she heard someone call out.

"Hey, you, in the blue hoodie. You're late for class."

Katie turned around and saw an eighth grader walking toward her. She had seen her before, but didn't know her name. The girl was half a foot taller than Katie and was wearing makeup. She looked old enough to be a high school student.

"Do you have a pass?"

"No, I was...taking care of something in the band room, and I didn't hear the last bell."

"That's no excuse. You have to go to the front office and get an admit slip."

"Oh, please, I'm already late and my class is right there," she said, pointing to Room 19. "I promise I won't be late again. Can I just go?"

"No, you can't." The eighth grader seemed pleased with herself at being able to discipline a pixie. "Office." She pointed in the opposite direction. "And hurry up."

Katie walked to the main office. She had never been late before and didn't know exactly where to go for an admit slip. Just as she was pulling open the back door, she saw a small sign that read "Admits, Room B1" with an arrow pointing left. There was another door to the left labeled B1. Katie opened it and stepped inside. The room was a small, windowless space, not connected to the main office. It looked like the ball closet at the elementary school. It was kinda dark in there, except for a small desk lamp on one of the two cubicle desks.

"Hello?" Katie called softly. "I... I need an admit slip." She waited. "Please."

There was a shuffling sound and a small, scaly head appeared over the cubicle edge. Another dragon. It had two black horns rising above its pale green forehead; the ears were large and tipped with white. The face was like an iguana, only uglier and its eyes were bright green. "Yesssss," it hissed at her.

"I'm late for Math and I need an admit slip."

"Why were you late?" asked the dragon, one clawed hand idly flipping through a stack of papers.

"I was at the band equipment room, taking care of something, and I didn't hear the bell." Katie wondered if she should mention the other dragon, but decided not to. She might get into more trouble.

"A likely story."

"Please, I have to get back to class."

"Well, were you acting on school business?"

"No, um...I..."

"Yes or no, only. I do not wish to hear your stories." The dragon's tongue flickered out of its mouth and Katie took a tiny step back from the desk. "Did a teacher send you?"

"No." Katie looked at its shiny black claws, which were now drumming on the table top, making an odd clicking noise, like a clock ticking.

"Do you have a written excuse from home?" The dragon looked down at the papers, and then back at Katie. "Did you have a doctor's appointment?"

"No, to both of those." Katie couldn't understand why she'd need a note from home to be in the band equipment room.

"Then there is no excuse. You are UNEXCUSED." The dragon turned its back and began filing the yellow half sheets of paper that were in a basket behind the desk.

"But I need an admit slip. I was just late for class." Katie gripped her backpack and wondered what Ms. Bernaschina was going to say when she showed up this late and without an admit slip.

"Too bad. Have an excuse next time. Now go." The dragon flicked one set of claws over its shoulder and continued filing.

Katie backed out of room B1 and headed to class. She hoped she wouldn't come across anyone who wanted to see her admit slip. She ran around the corner of the hall, but she didn't see the backpack just sitting in the middle of the way. She was going too fast to avoid it and tripped. Her hands flew out in front of her and she landed hard, a sharp pain running up through her arm. Katie cried out and rolled into a ball.

"Are you okay?" A woman's voice called out from further down the hall and Katie heard the click of high heels.

She looked up and saw Mrs. Gaderlund, the choir teacher, walking quickly toward her. She crouched down next to Katie.

"Can you stand up?"

"I think so." Katie tried to stand up, but felt wobbly. She put her hands out to steady herself and the pain in her right wrist made her wince even more.

"You should go and see the nurse." Mrs. Gaderlund patted her arms and shoulders, checking for damage. "You might have broken something. At least you should get your knee bandaged; it's bleeding."

Katie looked down at her torn jeans and skinned right knee. "I'm all right. I just fell."

"I know, I saw you trip over that Zuca and go flying. I keep telling Ms. Thompson that those things should be banned. They're a menace."

"I'm okay, really. Thanks, but I have to get to class," Katie picked up her bag and backed away, cradling her right wrist in her left hand and trying not to cry, but the pain was getting worse.

When she opened the classroom door, everyone looked at her. Ms. Bernaschina had a stern look on her face. Katie made her way through the rows of desks and sat down. The day
was going from bad to worse; Maia wasn't talking to her, the baby dragon was missing, Josh thought she was crazy, and now she was in trouble with Ms. B.

She tried to take her math notebook out of her backpack, but the motion made her wrist hurt even more. By now, it was throbbing with pain.

"Ms. Bernaschina?"

"Yes?" She had been writing problems on the board and turned to look at Katie.

"I fell down outside and I think I hurt my wrist."

"Oh, my. Did this happen just now? Is that why you were late?" Ms. Bernaschina walked over and lifted Katie's hand off the desk gently. "Where does it hurt?"

Katie pointed to a spot on her arm.

"Yes, It's starting to bruise. You should definitely go see the nurse."

Katie awkwardly collected her things and walked out of class. When she got out into the hallway, the tears started to fall. She was sniffing and her nose was dripping by the time she got to the office. The nurse gave her an ice pack and called her mother. Mrs. Walker took one look at Katie's wrist, which had started to swell and was really hurting by then, and took her to the emergency room. The x-rays showed that she'd broken a bone in her wrist and she had to have a cast. She chose a purple one. Finally, her mother took her home and she could rest. It had been a terrible day.

CHAPTER TEN
Dark of the Moon

Katie didn't see Maia at all for two days. Her mother kept her home the first day and then only let her go back to school if she skipped gym class, so she spent the time in the library. She didn't even know if Maia knew about her broken wrist.

On Friday, she wanted to get pizza for lunch, so she was waiting in line when Maia and Victoria walked up. They flashed 'front of the line' passes and went to the head of the line. Katie sighed. She had hoped to talk to Maia, but she didn't even notice her until she came out with her lunch.

"Hi, Katie. What happened to your arm?" Maia stopped and pointed at the cast.

"I was running for class, tripped over a backpack that was in the way, and I fell." She turned her arm around. "I broke my wrist."

"Does it hurt?"

"It aches a bit, but not too bad."

Just then, Victoria came up behind Maia. "What'd she do to her arm?"

"She tripped and fell," Maia said, before Katie could explain.

"What a klutz." Victoria said, and Maia laughed. Victoria started to walk away and pulled on Maia's sleeve. "Come on."

"Wait a second, Maia," Katie said. She wanted Maia to understand about her broken wrist, but Maia's attention was already on Victoria.

"I'll see you later," Maia said, walking away.

§

The next two weeks were torture. Having a broken wrist meant that she couldn't write with her normal hand; she couldn't play the flute; she seemed to have trouble with everything. Maia barely mumbled "hi" when they passed in the halls. She was spending every break and lunch with Victoria and a bunch of populars. Katie tried to join them a couple of times but the girls just talked around her as if she wasn't there, so she stopped trying.

Josh started coming and sitting with her at lunchtime, trying to help her with little things, like opening her water bottle. He never said a word about the dragons again, so she never mentioned it either. At least he was still talking to her.

She went to the locker room a few times to look for the baby dragon, but there was no sign of it. She even went to the library to see the Japanese dragon but she never found it, either. Now that it had its own library card, maybe it had moved to a different part of the school. Katie was feeling abandoned.

One afternoon, while she was studying in her room, Rosie barged in.

"Whatcha doing?" Rosie plopped down on Katie's bed.

"Math. Now get outta here."

"Where's Maia? She hasn't been over in a while."

"She's busy." Katie hadn't told anyone that they weren't speaking to each other. "So am I. Now leave."

"But she promised to take me to school to see one of the dragons."

"You can't."

"Why not?" Rosie had that look on her face, the one that said she wasn't leaving until she got what she wanted. Katie tried to ignore her, but she stepped closer to the desk and stamped one sneakered foot. "She promised."

"She's not here and besides, the dragons are all gone."

"I don't believe you. I think you just want to keep them to yourself."

Katie looked up. She had begun to wonder if she'd dreamed all the dragons. The big one in the band equipment closet, the blue-green water dragon, the baby, even the awful thing with black claws that handed out admit slips. She sighed and put her hand on Rosie's arm.

"Look, I'm not trying to be difficult. I haven't seen any dragons in a while and I think they may have left Graham."

"Where do you think they went?"

"I don't know, Rosie. You're the expert. Maybe you could look it up in your book."

"Okay." Rosie seemed satisfied with the new challenge and she left without another comment. Katie went back to her math homework.

Just before dinner, Rosie rushed into her room again, lugging several books. "I don't think they left. I think they're in hiding because of the new moon."

"What are you talking about?

"The dragons of Graham. See, it says here that dragons tend to go into hiding during the dark of the moon. Maybe they don't like the dark all that much."

"That doesn't make sense, Rosie. The first one I met was living in the dark equipment room."

"Well, I don't know why, but it says here that they don't like the dark of the moon. And I looked online and the new moon was yesterday, so that might explain it. But if that's true, then they should be around by the weekend."

Katie looked at her skeptically. She looked at the book that Rosie was holding open. It seemed to be some old almanac or something.

"Will you take me over there on Saturday? Please?" Rosie bounced on her toes.

"I don't know, Rosie."

"Please? Maia said she would and I really want to see a dragon."

"I'll think about it."

Their mother called them for dinner and the discussion ended for now. Neither of them wanted to talk about dragons in front of their parents.

CHAPTER ELEVEN
MUR Dragon

Katie forgot about Rosie's request the next day because she had so much homework. They had to create a model of the earth's crust for science class and she had an essay to write for language arts. The first draft was due tomorrow and she had no idea what her earth model was going to look like. Some kids made theirs out of styrofoam balls; Mr. Alberts showed them one made in a plastic tube. He said they could find materials at Michael's or the TAP Plastic store downtown. She wished she could talk it over with Maia and see what she was planning. Maia was always so creative when it came to building things.

They'd done several science fair projects together in elementary school; Maia designed the displays and Katie wrote up the results. They were a good team. Maybe Maia was teamed up with Victoria now. Katie didn't want to think about that.

Josh came and sat with her at lunch. "So how are you going to make your crust?" He took a bite of his sandwich. "I was thinking of doing it with polymer clays, you know, different colors for the different layers. Although I really wanted to make a 3D computer model. I think I need to talk to Mr. Sayer about that."

"I have no idea. It's a stupid project anyway."

"No, it's gonna be fun. Why are you in such a bad mood? Is your wrist hurting? Or is it that dragon thing?"

Katie looked at him, surprised that he'd even mentioned the dragons. "No, it's not the dragons, although my sister thinks they are all hiding because it's the dark of the moon."

"That would make sense. The lunar cycle has a profound influence on the earth, like tides and stuff."

She laughed. He was the first one who ever said the dragons made sense. "You think so?"

"Sure, why not?" He drank some milk. "So what about the crust model?"

"Well, that thing with the plastic tube seems pretty simple."

"Yeah, you could use different materials to make the

layers. You know, with different properties. Cause some of the layers are molten and some are dense rock. You could model that, too."

"Just no jello." Katie laughed. "Mr. Alberts was clear about that. He said it would just rot and smell bad."

§

Katie's mother took her to TAP Plastics after school and she decided to do something in a round plastic box that would look like a slice through the earth. She made a list of the different layers she had to make and tried to figure out what would look right. The middle, the magma, needed to be something red.

Katie had laid out all kinds of art supplies on her desk on Saturday morning. She had to get serious about this model. She had modeling clay, paint, glitter and paper. She thought about digging up some dirt from the edge of the driveway and maybe looking for some rocks at the park. Josh's idea about modeling the density sounded important. She didn't want to make something lame. But Mr. Alberts said that the scale was very important. They couldn't have rocks that were the size of planets inside the earth. Katie sighed. This was going to be harder than she expected.

Rosie opened the door and poked her head in. "Are you ready to go?"

"Go where?" Katie put down the list she had been staring at.

"School. You promised."

"What are you talking about?" Katie didn't remember making any promises to Rosie.

"The dragons. It's time to go look for dragons at Graham. They should have come out of hiding now that the new moon is waxing."

"Waxing? What the heck is waxing?" Katie imagined their dad waxing his car, only it was shaped like the moon.

"It means that the moon is getting fuller every night. After the full moon, it starts waning."

"Where do you learn these things?" Katie muttered as she turned back to the earth model. Maybe Josh could meet them at school and help her figure out what to use in the different layers. She wasn't getting anywhere by herself.

"Ok, give me a few minutes to make a phone call and then I'll take you."

Rosie ran out the door and down the hall, her blond hair flying.

Katie jammed on her sneakers and followed Rosie down the hall. She pulled the Graham phone list out of the spot where they kept it by the phone and dialed his number. Suddenly, she was nervous about talking to Josh on the phone, but it was all ready ringing.

"Hello?"

"Josh, it's Katie. Are you busy?"

"I was working on my science project."

"That's what I wanted to talk to you about. I'm having some trouble figuring out what to use for the layers. Can you meet me at school in a little bit and help me?"

"Sure. No problem. Where do you want to meet?"

"How about outside Mr. Alberts's room? And if he's there, we could go and talk to him, too."

"Good idea."

"Thanks." Katie hung up and went to tell her mother what they were going to do. She found her mom in the kitchen making cookies.

"Mom, I'm taking Rosie over to Graham for a bit. I have to meet a boy from science class to talk about the crust models. He's gonna help me. And Rosie wants to come, too."

Her mother gave her a look. Normally, she knew Katie didn't want to have Rosie anywhere near her. "Be careful crossing El Camino. And don't stay too long."

"Yes, ma'am. We'll be back in an hour at the most."

Rosie was already out front, bouncing up and down in the grass. When she saw Katie, she took off running in the direction of the middle school. Katie had to jog to keep up with her. They were across El Camino and onto the school grounds in no time. Rosie was suddenly shy when they crossed the parking lot beside the gym. The doors to the gym were locked, so looking for the baby dragon in the shower room was out. They passed the soccer field and Katie saw a flashing dark ponytail. Maia played forward on the sixth grade team and they were warming up. They probably had a game in a little while.

Rosie saw her, too, and started to run over to the field, but Katie held her back.

"Don't bother them. Maia's busy getting ready for a game."

"But I want to talk to her."

"Maybe later. We'll walk past after we go look around. I want to go to room 23 and see if Mr. Alberts is here." She didn't mention that they were meeting Josh. Rosie would just tease her about liking him or something.

"Does he have any dragons in his room?"

"No, silly. He's my science teacher. We'll look for dragons after that."

They walked past the library and the office. The little door where Katie had gone for an admit slip, B1, was closed and she didn't want to see that dragon again. He gave her the creeps. Katie turned down the row of classrooms. Room 23 was in the middle of the row on the right. The door was closed, but it was unlocked. They went in, but Mr. Alberts wasn't there. He must be around somewhere. Katie decided to look around at the models on the shelf while she was waiting for Josh to get here; maybe she would get some ideas about the crust layers. Ten minutes passed.

Suddenly Katie remembered Rosie. Where was she? She thought Rosie had followed her into the room, but she had been so wrapped up in looking at the models that she didn't check.

Katie looked around, but there was no place to hide, just rows of tables and chairs. She bent down and looked under the tables just to be sure. She didn't put it past Rosie to hide just so she'd have to look for her. Josh walked in, just as she stood up.

"Hi, Katie. Whatcha doing?"

"Looking for my little sister. She was here a minute ago."

"Maybe she went to the bathroom?"

Katie thought about where Rosie might have gone.

"Maybe she went out to the field to talk to Maia. We saw her there on the way in." She walked to the door and looked up and down the walkway outside. No sign of Rosie. "Would you mind going over there and seeing if she's there?"

"No, I mean, sure. I'll go ask Maia if she's seen her."

"And I'll go check the bathroom."

They left the classroom and went in opposite directions.

Katie headed to the bathrooms in the courtyard. They were empty. Coming out, she noticed that the door to the MUR was open a tiny bit. The Multi-Use-Room was their school auditorium. It looked more like a cafeteria, with a high ceiling and linoleum floor, but there was a stage at one end, with a big curtain. Maybe Rosie was in there, hiding.

Katie pulled open the door. The blinds over the high windows were closed and the room was dark. "Rosie?" She let the door close slowly behind her. She stood still, letting her eyes get adjusted to the dark. She didn't want to stumble around and knock over chairs.

As she stood there, she realized that the room wasn't completely silent. There were shuffling noises coming from the stage at the end of the room. She slowly moved in that direction, around the rows of metal folding chairs that she could just make out in the gloom. "Rosie?"

The shuffling noises got louder.

"Rosie, is that you? Come on out. I found you."

Sometimes Rosie could be so stubborn when she was playing a game and she wouldn't give in, even if she'd lost.

"You had me going there for a few minutes. I've looked all over the school." Maybe she could make her feel like she almost won her game of hide and seek. "Rosie?"

The shuffling was replaced with a weird rumbling sound, like a motorcycle engine starting. Katie had reached the stage end of the MUR by now. She stood still, trying to see exactly where the noise was coming from. It seemed to come from behind the stage curtain. She wasn't sure if Rosie was making the noise, but she had an idea.

One of the first days of school, Mr. Cassell had been showing them around and had taken them backstage, from the band-room side. There was a little hallway that led to the stage. He had pulled a rope to open the curtain while they were all standing there. She thought she could get to it from the side of the stage now. That would really surprise Rosie, to have the curtain open while she was hiding back there.

Katie tried to walk quietly up the little stairs to the side of the stage. She didn't want Rosie to come out and see her.

That would ruin the surprise. She slipped behind the edge of the curtain and felt along the wall in the darkness. The rope was somewhere. She found it and pulled it hard, hoping it wouldn't make too much noise. The rope stuck for a second and then began to move, and the curtain slid open. Katie ran back down the stairs so that she would be standing in front of the stage when the curtain finished opening and revealed Rosie, like magic.

It was still really dark in the MUR and she couldn't see anything as the curtain slowly moved across the stage.

"Rosie?" Katie whispered.

She was answered, not by her sister, but by a cough and a spout of flame. The flames were coming from an enormous, bronze dragon. He lay curled on the stage, reaching from edge to edge. The ridge of his back nearly touched the lights hanging above the stage and she could see the tip of his huge tail swishing back and forth on the wooden floorboards.

The loud rumble she'd heard before came again, from deep inside him. He turned his head in her direction and she could suddenly see Rosie, clutched in one of his front claws.

CHAPTER TWELVE
Captured

Katie gasped. Her sister was literally in the clutches of this enormous dragon. She had to do something. Maybe if he hadn't seen her, she would be able to sneak up on him somehow and get Rosie away from him. But she needed help. She slipped out of the MUR and headed for the soccer field. Josh had gone to ask Maia if she'd seen Rosie. Both of them knew about the dragons, even if Maia didn't want to talk about them anymore. She had to help her now. They had to save Rosie.

When Katie turned the corner of the last classroom building, she could see that the teams were taking a break.

Graham's soccer team was on the closer side of the field, standing around drinking from water bottles and laughing. Katie saw Josh talking to Maia, who was sitting on the ground, tying her shoe.

"Maia, Josh, I need your help." Katie crouched down beside the fence, her fingers laced in the mesh. She didn't want anyone else to hear them, so she whispered. "It's Rosie."

"Oh, you found her? Good." Josh walked over to where Katie was crouching. She stood up.

"No, no, it's not good. She's in trouble."

"What kind of trouble?" Maia joined them.

"There's a giant 'you-know-what' in the MUR, on the stage, and it has her in its claws."

"What 'you-know-whats'?" Maia asked, confused.

"Come on, Maia. You know." Katie lowered her voice even further and hissed out the word. "Dragons."

"Did you try to get her away from it?" Josh looked worried.

"Not yet. I need your help."

Maia looked over her shoulder at the team about to take the field. "I have a game."

"Maia, this can't wait. If we don't do something, Rosie's gonna get hurt. Maybe he's going to eat her. There were *FLAMES* coming out of his mouth."

"Flames? You didn't say anything about flames." Now Josh looked really worried.

"Yeah, flames. Come on. We have to get back there."

"Yeah, let's go. Rosie is more important than any game." Maia dropped her things and jumped the fence.

Katie whispered "Thank you." The three of them raced across the blacktop, down the hallway, and came to a stop just outside the MUR doors.

"So, do you have a plan?" Maia asked before they opened the door.

"Not really. I thought we'd talk to it, maybe we can convince it to give Rosie back."

"Talk to it?" Josh seemed confused.

"Well, it's too big to fight, and I don't have anything gold with me to tempt it. Do you?" Katie asked Maia.

"No," Maia said, "but we'll think of something."

Katie smiled at Maia. It was good to have her friend with her, even if it was for such a bad reason. They opened the MUR door, which squeaked on its hinges. The square of light from outside didn't do much to light up the room, but they could make out the dragon on the stage because of the small jets of flame that came from its nostrils with each breath.

They slipped inside and crept up to the stage along the side of the room. The dragon didn't notice them, because it was talking to Rosie and she was mad.

"I do NOT taste like sugarplums. That's just some story in a book. I don't taste good at all." Rosie banged her hands against the scaly skin of the dragon's claws. He had her securely pinned in his fist.

"Maybe not. However, I do not see why I should believe you." The dragon's voice was very deep and faintly foreign.

"I'm telling the truth."

"Rosie," Katie hissed. Both Rosie and the dragon turned and looked at the three kids standing by the stage.

"There you are, Katie" Rosie whined. "Maia, I've been trying to tell this big oaf that little girls don't taste good, but he says that we do. That we taste like sugarplums and spice and everything nice."

"That's just a nursery rhyme." Maia pointed out.

"That's what I told him, but he doesn't believe me." Rosie smacked his fist again. "He's planning to eat me."

Katie moaned. She knew it had been a bad idea to bring Rosie to look for dragons, she just didn't realize how bad. What were they going to do?

"Wait a minute," said Josh, suddenly. "Since he doesn't believe you, maybe we should have a little wager over it." Katie and Maia both looked at him. "You know, a bet."

"What kind of bet?" The dragon asked, joining the conversation for the first time.

"Well, how about a riddle contest?"

Josh leaned over to Katie and whispered, "I read somewhere that dragons love riddles. If we can beat him at this, we
can get Rosie back."

Josh sounded like he knew what he was doing,
although Katie didn't know how.

"Mmm, I like riddles," the dragon rumbled.

"But what if we don't beat him? I don't know very
many riddles." Katie wasn't sure it would work.

"I know a few," said Maia. "Come on, we have to try
something."

"Okay." Katie turned back to the dragon. "We challenge
you to a riddle contest. If we win, you have to let my sister
go."

"And if I win, I'm going to eat her." He answered.

"Um, I don't know about that." Maia said.

"Oh, but isn't that what this is all about?" The dragon
voice was smooth and hypnotic. "We are wagering if she is
going to be a tasty snack."

"Yes...I mean, no. She's not a tasty snack." Katie
answered. She looked at Maia with panic.

"Right," shouted Rosie from the dragon's fist. "You can
do it." She had a look of admiration on her face and Katie
didn't want to let her down. She especially didn't want Rosie
to be eaten by a dragon.

"It's decided, then," said the dragon. "You go first. Ask me a riddle."

"No," said Josh, "You have Rosie. You go first."

Katie's eyes got wide. "What if we can't answer it, on the first try?" she hissed at him.

"Relax, Katie. We need to see what kind of riddles he knows."

The dragon's stomach rumbled for a few minutes. He closed his eyes as he thought of a riddle. "All right.

"What always runs, but never walks?
"What often murmurs, never talks?
"What has a bed but never sleeps?
"What has a mouth but never eats?"

Josh laughed. "That's easy. A river."

The dragon grumbled and Rosie cheered. Katie patted his arm. She hadn't expected him to know one so quickly.

"My turn," Maia said.

"Once there was a green house.
Inside the green house,
there was a white house.
Inside the white house,
there was a red house.

Inside the red house,
there were lots of babies.
What is it?"

Katie knew the answer and she was sure the dragon must know it, too.

He answered without a pause. "A watermelon." A little flame shot out of his mouth. Katie wondered if he was going to set the curtains on fire that way. "I must think of something harder." He hummed for a few minutes.

Katie leaned into Maia. "Do you really know a lot of riddles?"

"Sure, don't you?"

"No. Well, maybe a few."

"Good. Think of them and we'll take turns. You can go next."

The dragon opened his eyes and glared at them. "I doubt you will answer this one." He took a deep breath and rumbled again.

"Each morning I appear,
to lie at your feet,
"All day I will follow you,
no matter how fast you run,
"Yet I nearly perish in the midday sun."

Katie, Josh and Maia put their heads together. "Do you think it's a dog? That would lie at your feet and run as fast as you can."

"No, but it wouldn't perish in the midday sun."

"Oh, wait. I get it." Kate lifted her head and looked straight at the dragon. "Is it a shadow?"

"Yes." The dragon's voice rumbled even lower. He sounded disappointed that she had guessed correctly. Maia and Rosie clapped for Katie.

"Now, I'll tell you one." She balled up her fists and said it slowly so that she didn't mess it up.

"What's in the sun but not in the moon,
"What's in a song, but not in a tune,
"Out in the days, but gone at night,
"Out of reach, but still in sight?"

"Oh, that's a good one," said Rosie. She tried to climb up in the dragon's fist. He had relaxed his claws a little as they were playing the riddle contest, but now he squeezed her tight again. "Ouch, that hurts."

"Be still, little girl. I have to think." The dragon twisted his head around until it was facing away from them while he tried to figure out the riddle. The kids waited for several minutes.

"Come on, Mr. Dragon. If you don't know the answer, admit it." Josh called out.

"I'm still thinking," rumbled the dragon.

"We'll give you one more minute." Maia made a show of looking at her watch. She was pressing the little button on the side to turn the light on. As the second hand swept around, she began to count down. "Thirty.....twenty-five.....twenty...."

The dragon turned back toward them. "Hush, I can't think with you nattering like that."

"Fifteen seconds....Sir."

Katie and Josh joined her in the countdown."Ten...nine ...eight...seven...six...five...four..."

"The letter S." The dragon had answered just in time. The kids all groaned. The dragon laughed. "Now I have a hard one for you.

"I am always hungry,
I must always be fed,
The finger I touch,
Will soon turn red."

He laughed a smug laugh.

Katie whispered with Maia again. "Do you know that one?"

"No, I don't but we should be able to figure it out. What is hungry and has to be fed? A mouth? A baby?"

"Maybe, but those won't turn a finger red, until they bite you. Do you think that's it?" Katie didn't want to answer too soon. If they got it wrong, they would lose the contest and the dragon would eat her sister. "We have to be really sure."

"He didn't say anything about biting. It was 'the finger I touch.' So what can turn red with just a touch?" Josh asked.

"Paint? Or maybe something juicy, like a strawberry?" Maia was running out of ideas.

"No, I don't think so." Josh looked up at the dragon, just as he shot another burst of flame out of his nose. "That's it."

"What?"

"Fire. See what he just did? I know that's it." Josh spoke loud enough for the dragon to hear. "The answer is fire."

"Yes, yes it is." He was beginning to sound angry that they were able to guess his riddles.

Now it was Katie and Rosie's turn to cheer.

"Your turn," said the dragon in a menacing voice. "And hurry. I'm getting hungry." He lifted Rosie a foot off the stage.

"Put her down." Katie climbed up on the stage and stood

right in front of the dragon. "You made a deal and you better

keep it. I have one more riddle for you." She put her hands on her hips and stuck out her chin. "This one is short."

"How far will a blind man walk into a forest?"

"Hmmm, I don't think I've heard that one before. Let me think."

"Well, don't take too long. I'm watching the time." Maia said, as she held up her watch.

"Rosie, are you okay?" Katie stepped closer to her sister. The dragon didn't seem to be paying attention.

"Yes. Well, except for this." She pointed to the claws wrapped around her middle.

"How did he catch you? I was looking at the science projects and all of a sudden you were gone."

"I got tired of waiting for you, so I went looking around. I heard something in the auditorium and the door was open, so I came in. I thought it might be a good place for a dragon to hide, and I was right."

"Yeah, but he wants to eat you. Doesn't sound too good to be right, does it?"

"No..." Rosie looked a little scared now, not as mad as she was earlier.

"We'll get you out of here, don't worry. Maia, how much time?" Katie looked over her shoulder at her friend.

"It's been three minutes."

"Okay, Mr. Dragon, we need your answer."

The dragon opened his eyes again. He looked from Maia to Josh to Katie. "I think it's a trick question. I mean, how would a blind man know he's in the forest?"

"It's not a trick question." Katie began to hope that they might have stumped him.

"No? Then let me think about it some more."

This made her mad. "No more thinking. If you don't know the answer, just say so."

"Well, tell me what the answer is, then. How far will a blind man walk into a forest?"

"Half-way." Katie smiled. "After he gets half way, he's walking OUT of it. Now let my sister go."

Katie reached out and pulled Rosie by the hand. The dragon's claws had relaxed enough at this point that Rosie was able to slip out. Katie tightened her grip and jumped off the stage, bringing Rosie with her. Josh caught them before they tumbled to the floor. "Let's go."

The kids turned and raced for the door just as the dragon realized that he had lost both his contest and his snack. He let out a roar, with a long jet of flame, just as they pulled the door open and ran through. Maia was the best runner of the group and she pulled ahead across the courtyard and down a row of classrooms. Josh was right behind. Katie was still holding on to Rosie's arm and didn't want to pull her off balance. They were slower. Katie could hear the doors bang open behind them and caught a glimpse of the dragon's head following them just as she turned the corner.

He was coming after them. She had to get Rosie out of there, before they were both fried to a crisp and eaten for lunch. She tried to run faster, but she could feel her grip on Rosie slipping. Maia disappeared beyond the row of classrooms, just as Rosie stumbled, and Katie lost her grip. Rosie fell flat on her face, and cried out as she scrapped her hands and knees on the rough cement.

"Rosie," Katie yelled. "Josh, help me." Katie turned and ran back to her sister.

The dragon had cleared the courtyard and turned in to the row of classrooms. It was the first time that Katie could really see him. He was huge and covered in scales, the sun glinting off his dark bronze skin. His claws were each almost a foot long and he moved with a speed and grace that Katie didn't know was possible for something that big. He didn't lumber like an elephant, he nearly flew, even though Katie couldn't see if he had wings or not.

Josh reached them and tried to lift Rosie up and carry her but she was crying and struggling. She was too heavy for him to carry and Katie knew they were not going to be able to outrun the dragon. She crouched over Rosie to protect her. It was all she could think of. Just as she bent her head, so she wouldn't have to watch the flames come toward them, she heard a loud voice.

"Subsisto! Audite meus to order. Vado tergum ut vestri cubile."

Katie raised her head in shock. The dragon was backing away and grumbling, but he was going. She looked back toward the voice.

There stood Mrs. Mitchell with her hand out, pointing at the dragon, like it was a bad dog. The dragon turned and glided away. Mrs. Mitchell walked up to Katie and helped her lift Rosie to her feet. She put her arm around Josh's shoulder.

"Well, children, I think that's enough excitement for now. How about a cup of hot chocolate?"

Katie and Josh just stared at her. Rosie was the first one to respond.

"I want some." Rosie wiped the tears off her face. "Come on, Katie." She took Katie's hand and they followed Mrs. Mitchell back to her classroom.

Josh looked back over his shoulder and then asked Mrs. Mitchell, "What did you say to him?"

"Oh, that? Just a little Latin, telling him to stop and go back to where he came from."

Maia came running back around the corner of the building, just as they got to the door to Mrs. Mitchell's classroom. She was gasping for breath, with tears running down her face. "Are you all right? What happened? I thought you were right behind me, but then you weren't."

"It's okay, Maia. Mrs. Mitchell stopped the dragon for us." Rosie said. "Come have some hot chocolate."

CHAPTER THIRTEEN
The Dragon Lady

They sat in a circle of desks in Mrs. Mitchell's room while she made them some hot chocolate with her kettle. Rosie told her all about looking for the dragons, being captured, and their riddle contest with the big dragon. "And Katie stumped him and rescued me."

"That was very good thinking on your part, Katie."

"Well, the riddle contest was Josh's idea. And Maia knew the most riddles." Katie explained.

"Yeah, but Katie came up with the winning riddle." Maia added.

Katie smiled at the look of appreciation on Maia's face. It felt like her friend was really back with her again.

"Mrs. Mitchell, how did you know about the dragon?" Josh asked.

She was smiling as she put down her mug of hot chocolate. "Why do you think they call me the Dragon Lady?"

Maia, Josh and Katie burst out laughing.

"I thought that was just a name....for...you know...being old." Katie blushed as she said it.

"Actually, it's a title. I'm responsible for all the dragons at Graham. I wish I'd known that you were looking for them before this. I could have saved you a lot of trouble."

"We didn't just start looking today," Katie said. She wasn't sure how much she should admit.

"No, we found the first one, or really Katie found the first one, at the beginning of school." Maia said, without any hesitation.

"It was in the band equipment room."

"Ah, yes. He's a young one and he likes all those silver band instruments."

"Tell her about the others." Rosie didn't want to be left out of the conversation. "They asked me questions about that one and the water dragon and..."

"Wait, wait. Ladies, you seem to know quite a bit about the dragons of Graham. Maybe you'd better start from the beginning." She opened her desk drawer and took out a map of the school with some markings on it.

"There's a map?" Josh asked, surprised.

After all, he'd only seen the big dragon today. He was still getting used to the idea.

"Of course. We have to keep track of them somehow."

"Well, you have a new one to add." Katie said. "Did you know about the egg we found in Maia's locker?"

"An egg? No. That's odd. I didn't know any of the dragons were in season. All right. Tell me about the egg. What did you do with it? You weren't there when it hatched, were you?" She sounded alarmed.

"I was, but I covered my face so that it wouldn't imprint on me." Katie was proud of herself for knowing that. "I was trying to carry the egg to the girls' locker room when it started to crack. After it hatched, I lured it with grapes and pieces of my tuna fish sandwich. I thought it might want to be with the water dragon who lives in the shower room."

"That's a good idea. A very good idea. Chinese Lungs are very helpful and thoughtful. Yes, I think they will get along very well." Mrs. Mitchell made a mark on the map.

"Mrs. Mitchell, is the water dragon all right? I was really worried, because he doesn't seem to have enough water. He came after my water bottle once, like he was really thirsty."

"Oh, that one's a female and she does like bottled water. The PE teachers usually run the showers for her every few days, but I'll ask them about it. Make sure she's okay." She made another note. "I'm going to have to make you children my assistants, I think."

Maia and Katie grinned and gave each other a high five. Josh looked a little stunned.

"What about me?" Rosie asked.

"What grade are you in?" Mrs. Mitchell asked.

"Second." Rosie stuck out her bottom lip. "But I know more about dragons than these two."

"Well, I think we can work something out, and then when you come to Graham, you will know more than anyone here. Except me, of course."

"Okay." Rosie brightened. She seemed to like the idea of being a dragon expert.

The kids all raised their mugs in a toast. "To the dragons of Graham."

The End

Acknowledgments

Bringing a book to life takes more than just an imagination and time. It takes the support of many folks. I'd like to thank Heather Haven, my literary partner, for all her wise words, hard work, and strong support.

I want to thank the many people who gave me feedback on this story, including Susy, Bradley, Tony, Robert, Thida, Elizabeth, Katy, Mary, Tracy, Herb, Liza, Yvonne, and members of the Orcas 9. I also want to thank to Ellen Sussman for her support of my work.

Thank you, Dylan, for the dragon art, and Jeff, for help with the cover.

Many thanks to all the administration, faculty and staff of Graham Middle School, for making our time there so wonderful. This book is, in part, an effort to capture what is so special about the school.

Finally, thanks to my family for making the effort possible.

About the Author

Baird Nuckolls is a writer, literary editor, mom, and a jack-of-many trades. She has been in charge of all the Performing Arts bake sales at Graham for the past six years. This is her first middle grade novel.

Brought to you by

The Wives of Bath Press

www.thewivesofbath.com

Made in the USA
Charleston, SC
22 February 2013